Inner Core

About the author

Miki Lentin took up writing while travelling the world with his family a few years ago. He completed an MA in Creative Writing at Birkbeck in 2020 and was a finalist in the 2020 Irish Novel Fair for his first book *Winter Sun*. He has been placed highly in competitions including *Fish Publishing* and *Leicester Writes* and has been published in *Litro*, *Storgy*, *Story Radio*, *MIR* amongst others. Miki volunteers with foodKIND in Greece, and dreams of one day running a café again.

For more information, you can visit:
www.mikilentin.net/my-writing

"Miki Lentin's short stories are always consistently enthralling. I've loved the way that they have drawn me into painful, familiar male experiences. In particular, they explore men's emotions and troubled relationships in an honest, original and entertaining way. I can't stop turning the pages when I settle down to read them. They are funny, moving and disturbing in equal measure. They slice through contemporary life and expose the underbelly of what is really going on unconsciously, but are always framed by enlivening action and drama. Very highly recommended!"

Francis Gilbert, Head of the MA in Creative Writing and
Education at Goldsmiths University, author of
I'm a Teacher Get Me Out of Here and *The Last Day of Term*

"Miki Lentin takes linear time and smashes it to pieces, reassembling the shards as narrative mosaics. There is beauty, sadness, love, loss in the fragments but you need to stand back and take it all in to appreciate the bigger picture."

Lynda Clark, author of the short story collection
Dreaming in Quantum and *Beyond Kidding*

"With delicacy, Lentin lets the most ordinary items and details – a rock, clothes that smell of bread, meringues, a café mess, a butter dish – to suggest larger, more nuanced and complex feelings and perceptions. There is an admirable urgency, authenticity and grim humour throughout these stories."

Gerry Stembridge, author of *The Effect of Her*,
co-writer of the film *Nora* and the crime comedy
Ordinary Decent Criminal

"Miki's stories about working with refugees are sensitively observed and moving - and they will enrich your understanding of an ethically complex subject."

Daniel Trilling, journalist and author of
Lights in the Distance and *Bloody Nasty People*.

About the story Inner Core:
"Great opening paragraph. Narrative slides effectively in and out of time, and the voice feels authentic."

David Shields, author of *Reality Hunger,*
The Thing About Life Is That One Day You'll Be Dead and
The Trouble With Men

Inner Core

Short Stories by Miki Lentin

Afsana Press
London

First published in 2022
by Afsana Press Ltd, London
www.afsanapress.uk

Typeset in Minion Pro / Garamond by Afsana Press Ltd

A CIP catalogue record for this book
is available from the British Library

ISBN: eBook: 978-1-7399824-3-0
Paperback: 978-1-7399824-4-7

All the proceeds from the sales of this book will go to the refugee charity
foodKIND, that supports refugees and vulnerable groups in crisis on the
mainland of Greece, providing food for over 700 people every day. Since
May 2016, foodKIND has served almost 1 million meals and is committed
to doing everything it can to make sure that in the places they work, no one
goes hungry. To donate and to find out more visit: www.foodkind.org

For Arielle and Eden.

Contents

PART I

Inner Core

I never admitted it to my wife M, but I really wanted the boy with the toothy grin to pull the trigger and shoot the French woman who was standing a few steps from us. I had nothing against her, I didn't want her to die. But at that moment, I wanted everything to pause, so I could hear the crack of a gun blast, smell the gunpowder, and see if I could follow the bullet spinning through the air. I even considered what it would be like to lick the spattered blood from my face, wipe M's jacket down, and go for dinner on the Asian side of Istanbul, just as we'd planned.

Lying awake back home in Dublin a few months later, I pondered this, as images of that evening flickered in my mind. Dizzy, my breath shallow, the small of my back tight, I fumbled in the dark for my watch, just like I did every night, knocking my hand into a book and a glass of water. It wasn't there, of course it wasn't.

I was sure that my watch had been stolen from our hotel room in Istanbul, on the last day of a city break M and I had taken. I knew that I'd wound the silver winder, which kept the mechanism faintly ticking just before I'd gone to bed. I knew that I'd placed it by the side of my bed, the strap doubled over, so I could see the watch face. I knew that I'd reached for it first thing in the morning, but for some reason hadn't put it on. I knew after breakfast that it was gone.

"My watch, have you seen it?" I'd yelled, my heart palpitating with panic.

"What?" she'd shouted from the shower. "Didn't you leave it by the bed?"

I spent what seemed like hours tossing clothes, opening cupboard doors, rummaging in bags, chucking sofa cushions, and retracing my steps around the hotel. While I searched, I kept touching my wrist, as if I could still feel the silver strap pinching the hairs on my arm.

It had been my father's Tissot, the watch my mother had placed on my wrist the day after he'd died. The hotel manager shrugged when I suggested that it might have been stolen. I didn't want to spoil M's birthday trip, and at some stage she held me tight and told me to stop, "just stop bloody looking." Reluctantly, I called the search off. "It's only a watch, these things are replaceable," I'd said, trying to convince myself.

Eyes wide open in Dublin, my spine pinching the nerves in my back like a bulldog clip, I looked at the LED alarm clock that M had bought me. It lit my pillow. Four a.m. She'd told me that it softened the light in the room, and was scientifically proven to assist sleep. I'd thanked her as I knelt down to plug it in, unable to bend my stiff spine, but I hated the digital display, and couldn't fathom why it also needed to show the room temperature.

I had woken at the same time every night for the past three or four months, but had lost track of just how long it had been.

My head, like an alarm clock, was set on repeat. Automatically it switched on a light in my mind, dropped the stylus of a turntable onto a vinyl record and started to play 'Breathe', that song by Pink Floyd, and filled my ears with the ticking of the kitchen clock. I put my lack of sleep down to encroaching age – nearing my fifties – and theorised that even though I might never get used to it, the older I got, the less sleep I needed.

A few weeks before, over curry and pints of lager, my friends all bemoaned their sleeplessness, citing anxious children, work worries and marriage difficulties, as they snapped poppadums and drenched them in chutney. I listened in, encouraged that I wasn't the only one not sleeping. I nodded in agreement, and took long gulps of beer. "Sure I read the other day that a pint every night actually helps you sleep," I said. We laughed, clinked glasses, and slapped each other on the back. I went home tipsy and happy, believing my lack of sleep was a phase. It would pass.

When M asked if I was tired, I'd shrug. Tired was not a word I used anymore. Resigned, maybe. Pissed off, perhaps. Scared, a little. I let my beard grow heavy, hoping it would mask my puffy eyes that squinted permanently. My left eyelid often twitched uncontrollably, and horseshoes circled my sockets like burn marks.

Some sleep guru called Yoram Schultz, who featured on a sleep masterclass app I'd bought, confidently informed me in a Californian drawl that a human can function fine on five or even four hours sleep a night. It was all in the "quality of the sleep you get," Yoram would say, "not the quantity." Every class would end with a mantra, "fill your whole being with breath, stay afloat, come home," and my favourite, "ride the mysterious sea," as if I had any idea what that meant.

Needing eight hours of shut-eye was a myth, I was informed, perpetuated by marketing people who didn't understand the physiological science behind sleep. Everything was scientific these days. Maybe I just didn't understand the science either. That was the problem. I had to become better informed. I read a bestseller about sleep that warned of early dementia if I didn't go to bed early, that I'd lose weight if I slept properly, and that more sleep would improve my looks. I listened to podcasts and read articles, did a mindfulness course, and an hour of hot yoga looking at some fella's sweaty arse bent over in front of me every Wednesday morning. But I kept putting the milk in the larder, had to strain my eyes wide when I drove to the supermarket, and couldn't concentrate when I read, often falling asleep at my desk at work.

And then there was the time I drove into the back of another car. "What the fuck! Like what the actual fuck!" the other driver screamed through the window as I nervously got out of the car to inspect the damage. "I'm really sorry, is, everyone ok?" I asked, even though I knew full well that there was barely anything wrong with her car, I was only going three miles an hour, and why was she being so obnoxious, and sure these things happen all the time, and I'd only closed my eyes for a split second before impact, so there was no way she could blame me for being negligent, and couldn't she just leave me alone and not make a fuss on the main road for God's sake, it was only a scratch.

I'd cower in a corner of the train every day on my way to work, my body battered with exhaustion. Fuelled by coffee, I was bombarded with adverts selling the ultimate spring-loaded

4

mattress with added this and that membrane which improved the airflow in bed, foam pillows that memorised the shape of my head, silk eye masks and silicone ear plugs that blocked out the world. Every night I put on the eye mask and ear plugs that came free with my new mattress topper. "Now then," I'd implore them eagerly before listening to an eleven o'clock sleep story on the app, "please help me sleep tonight." But when I wore them, I felt as if I was floating awake underwater, my heartbeat the only audible sound reverberating inside my hollow body.

It was jeans and t-shirt weather in Istanbul when M and I had visited, even though it was November. Wearing my cowboy hat and sunglasses, I held her hand as we roamed the antique shops and cafés of Kadiköy, drank muddy Turkish coffee, smoked like teenagers, drank a bit too much, and listened to schmaltzy jazz in a bar into the small hours. For those few days a lightness swept over me, like I was experiencing it for the first time.

The afternoon before we left for our last supper, we visited the Museum of Innocence, which was based on a book with the same name by the author Orhan Pamuk. I usually found the heaviness of historic museums tiring. I didn't always know where to start, and couldn't resist my childhood tendency to just look at the biggest and oldest pieces. The Museum of Innocence was different – four floors in a narrow house packed with objects all touched at one time by Fusun, a woman the narrator Kemal was obsessed with.

1,593 lipstick stained cigarette butts nailed to a board, smoked by Fusun and collected by Kemal, faded family photos in plastic albums, birth and death certificates written in curly handwriting, chipped wine glasses, the nibbled lids of pens, tarnished ornate silver cutlery, airmail letters with yellowing stamps, souvenir fridge magnets, empty bottles of perfume, crystal ashtrays, receipts stapled to accountancy booklets, floral dresses and shirts on hangers, an airgun, a set of rusty kitchen knives. Fusun's whole life, everything she had ever touched, in one house.

The soothing voice of the narrator on the audio guide told stories of Kemal's often daily visits to Fusun's house. I liked the way every item had a place, a role in the story. Nothing was wasted. I could press pause on the audio guide, and step inside Kemal's head at any moment in his life and his relationship with Fusun, and know what was going on. Each scene was documented in detail, with a beginning, middle and end. I wished I could pause and look into my own life like that. Chop it up, divide it, day by day, hour by hour, second by second, unblended.

Along the fourth-floor banister of the museum staircase, from where I could look down into the atrium, was a display unit with dozens of watches all collected by Fusun. Wrist watches, pocket watches, flip watches, alarm clocks. Some worked, some didn't. I spotted a silver watch that looked like my father's. It had those Roman numerals that glowed in the dark, which even at my age I thought was cool. My eyes looked up to the corners of the gallery to see if the security cameras were on me. I was almost sick with desire for the watch. I placed my elbows firmly on the glass of the cabinet, hoping it might crack. An empty retch pulled inside my guts. Maybe I could grab the watch. Maybe I could clip it onto my wrist. Maybe I could walk out without anyone noticing. I licked my lips in anticipation. Why, I thought, if Kemal needed to obsessively collect Fusun's belongings, couldn't I also take something that wasn't mine?

"Come on, let's go for dinner," M said, startling me.

"One minute," I said, and just before I left, I knelt down, put my ear to the glass, and concentrated on listening to the watch faintly ticking in the background.

I'd planned that we should visit the Asian side for our last dinner in Istanbul. We ran onto the passenger boat from the European port of Beyoğlu just as the barriers went up, sat on the side deck, shared a cigarette, and watched as a blue darkness enveloped the Bosphorus bay, silhouetting the minarets. The boat gurgled white frothy foam from its rear. I thought that it looked like an inviting bubble bath. The sea was now oily black and container ships and tankers blocked the view north to the Black Sea, and south to the Sea of Marmara. I liked the word Marmara. I liked trying to roll the r's. It sounded faraway and exotic.

We'd run out of mobile phone data and stood by the ticket machines in Kadiköy harbour on the Asian side, trying to connect to Wi-Fi so we could find somewhere to eat. Passenger boats came and went, moorings and gangways thrashed on piers, and people gathered and dispersed in the square around us. M said she was cold, so I slung my jacket over her shoulders. I fidgeted in the pockets of my jeans. It was getting late. As we scrolled through our mobile phones, out of the corner of my eye I saw a teenage boy approach a couple who were standing in front of the ticket machines for the boats. The boy was wearing tracksuit bottoms and a black hoodie with sleeves that had been ripped off at the elbow. He had a goofy

7

smile on his face, was nibbling his fingernails, and seemed to be bouncing on his feet.

Four-thirty a.m. in Dublin. My bloated bladder ached. The toilet was en-suite, and even though I never woke M, I didn't want to move. She slept like the dead. Her sleep ebbed and flowed like a calm river. Flicks of her arm after she dropped off, then a bit of chatting away to herself, the odd grunt and heavy breathing and then absolutely nothing. I felt calm looking at her while she slept, a picture of stillness, beauty, sculpture-like. I was desperate though, and sat on the toilet, my belly hanging over my waist, my spine throbbing with pain, and peed in the dark.

I turned onto my side and tried to hold my stomach in so it didn't flop onto the mattress. Aiden, my physiotherapist, had told me to clench my core. An MRI scan had shown that I had a bulging disc in my spine. My hip flexors screamed, the small of my back stretched like a tight-fitting jumper. Some days I hobbled straight-legged around the house, my legs with a mind of their own, holding onto the sink as I brushed my teeth, and kneeling on the floor to stack the dishwasher.

"Hold it now Jerry. Holding it will protect your core, but Jesus, don't forget to breathe now," Aiden laughed. "You can't do much if you don't breathe." I nodded as I forcefully exhaled.

"Protect your inner core," Aiden repeated, opening his mouth wide as he spoke, so I could see his uvula swinging like a jelly bean at the back of his throat.

Aiden instructed how I should hold my pelvic floor muscle: "Ten percent now, and don't hold your breath," so that my stomach didn't bulge. "Just a little now, concentrate now, slow down those exercises, it's all in the quality, not the quantity, that's what I want to see."

As Aiden used his pointy fingers to rub some oily muck into the small of my back, he gave me a running commentary of his drive to the gym in his new BMW. I didn't care. "Now remember, those deep inner connected muscles hold everything together," Aiden said.

I lay face down, wincing through the hole in the ripped paper sheet on the massage table. As I counted the tiles on the floor, the voices of the couple who stood next to M and me in Istanbul filled my head. They'd been arguing in French about which boat to get. She was striking and tall, long-legged and wearing high heels. Her hair waved onto her face in the breeze, and she was wearing what looked like a man's work shirt with a pink collar. Her companion was shorter than her. His white creased trousers stood out in the dark light and I noticed an ivory tooth pendant hanging from his neck.

It was five a.m. in Dublin. My mouth was parched, my lips dry. I knew that if I wasn't asleep by five-thirty, my chances of sleeping that night were low and, even if I did drop off, I'd wake suddenly again at seven and feel like a bomb had detonated in my head.

I bent my knees on my side of the bed and dropped my hips to one side, then the other, as Aiden had taught me. Lying still, my sore body now didn't want to move, as if the memory foam mattress topper remembered that I couldn't sleep. The brittle vertebrae of my spine rubbed together like stones, and my sciatic nerve shot spasms into my thighs and buttocks. Sometimes I visualised a scalpel slicing my flesh, and a doctor pouring liquid

9

painkiller into my body to numb the pain.

I lifted my buttocks into a bridge position. M turned to face me. Making her out in the dark, I looked at her closely, my arse in the air, wondering if she was looking at me. Her eyes were closed, the curls of her hair resting playfully on her forehead. Trying to loosen the tension in my back, I tucked my pelvis forward and back, holding my inner core as I worked.

"Can't you sleep, hon?" she asked sleepily.

"What?" Was I dreaming? "I thought you were asleep," I whispered.

"I am," she said, and reached out her hand to my body. It was warm, like a bowl heated by soup. She rested it on my shoulder for a few moments and turned over, taking the duvet with her.

'*Breathe, breathe in the air…*' That bloody song. I was breathing, but not deeply. I didn't breathe deeply anymore. Breathe, I told myself, breathe, concentrate on your breath, just like Elaine, the mindfulness teacher with the twinkly braces on her teeth had taught me. "Be gentle with yourself," she said. "Quality of the breath now, quality, not quantity. Slow down. Inhale. One, two, three, pause." She enunciated each word exactingly. "Hold it there. Exhale, three, two, one. Don't force it," she said, her smile lingering on me.

I practised my new breathing exercises every morning on my way to work, sometimes when I got home, when I went to the toilet, at my desk at work, often in the car and when I was watching television next to M on the sofa. But my breath was syrupy and thick, and even when I forcefully inhaled, it would get stuck half-way down my lungs, as if my windpipe was blocked.

I wriggled and twisted, turned over my pillows and threw

away my side of the duvet. I turned my head to face the LED alarm clock. Five-thirty a.m. I stared for what seemed like minutes at the circular lampshade that hung from the ceiling, until I thought I was floating from the ceiling looking at myself.

Thinking some fresh air would help, I got out of bed, opened the sliding doors to the garden, and let my feet freeze on the paving stones. Lying down, the cold stone numbed my back as a few drops of rain dribbled down my bare chest and dotted my boxer shorts. I looked up at the red sky, but all I could see were images of the teenage boy in Istanbul nonchalantly removing the gun from the pocket of his hoodie. The boy slowly straightened his right arm, held the gun at shoulder height and placed his left arm onto his right shoulder. Wrapping his forefinger around the trigger, his thumb rested lightly on the hammer as he bent his head slightly to the right so that he was now looking down the length of his arm, the barrel pointed directly towards the head of the woman.

A wailing siren nearby broke the silence in the garden. Empty and bereft, I looked at the skeletons of dead plants in pots spread around the patio, broken and battered from the winter chill. I wanted to cry, but as I tried, my head blisteringly cold, the rain got heavier, so I laboured up, and returned to the soothing warmth of lying next to M's body.

I closed my eyes. My head danced and spun around my bedroom. Could I smell roasted chestnuts from the Istanbul seafront? Tiny flashbulbs exploded in my mind. I felt as if my body was being knocked by people pushing past M and me to get to the ticket machines. Yoram appeared in a science lab coat bouncing on my bed singing that Pink Floyd song. The boy with the gun came into focus. "Ride the mysterious sea," Yoram read to me from an over-sized science manual. Aiden pushed Yoram out of the way. The boy moved stealthily closer to the French woman. "Protect your inner core, quality, not quantity…" Aiden cackled and shrieked. The boy didn't flinch, a broad grin across his face. The ticking of the kitchen clock got louder. The boy's arm was steady and strong. I covered my ears. The boy's legs shuffled sideways closer to the woman. I knelt next to the watch display in the museum. Nails dug into my back. The boy cocked his gun, just as the watches from the display cabinet in the Museum of Innocence all started to tick out of time in different tones to the beat of the song that never ended. "Go on," I muttered, willing the boy on, as if he was in my bedroom, "go on."

I opened my eyes. I dared not look at the alarm clock. I dared not look at the temperature of the room. I dared not look at M.

"*Jesus, Jerry!*" It was M who screamed first. The boy now stood directly in front of the couple.

"I can't sleep," I said, gripping the duvet to my chin.

"*What is it?*"

"I know love, I hear you getting up every night."

"*That fella, there, he's got a fucking gun!*"

"Sorry, I don't mean to wake you."

"*Don't, please!*" the French woman shouted.

"You don't, not every night. Are you still finding it hard to sleep?"

"*Please, put it down, it's no joke, OK?*"

"I've tried everything."

"*Help!*"

"Can I do anything to help?"

"*Please. Please. Don't.*"

"I don't know what to do anymore."

"*Do you want money? Here, I'll give you my watch, please…*"

"Are you still thinking about your father's watch?"

The Rock

Come on, come on, answer, I mouthed. Hello, Maxol Station, Swords Road, a voice said. Hi there. I… ehhh… was wondering if you could help me. Yeah? I'm looking for a rock. A what? A rock. We left it by the hoover machine. When? Yesterday. Can you have a look and see if it's still there, please? I'll have to speak to the manager. Is he there? He's on his break. It's white. What is? The rock. It's the size of a mini rugby ball, and it's quartz. OK, can you call back later?

*

The day before.

You have to get rid of the rock, I said. What? My teenage child asked. That's not what you said earlier. I did. I said that we'd have to lose it before we got to the airport. There's no way we'll get a rock of that size past security, OK? No you didn't. You said that you'd check online to see what's allowed on board and what's not allowed and obviously you haven't done that, as you never do what you say you're going to do. And now I feel like a bad parent,

14

the worst, because I haven't checked online. What would I even look up? Can you take a rock on board a plane? Well, it's too late now, I said, I have to finish cleaning the sand from the car and fill up and we still have to drive two k to the airport and it's already half past. We have to go. It's not my fault we're running late. I didn't say it was. Well, why are you still cleaning the car? So we don't get fined. Look, it says it there. Drivers who return cars with sand in them will be fined a hundred Euro. All I said was that you have to get rid of the bloody rock.

I stooped down, my head filling with blood now buried under the steering wheel, the ribbed tube of the petrol station hoover zipping against the car door, and vacuumed the fuzzy carpet, watching specks of sand fly into the air like tiny comets. Briefly, I came up for air and saw you gripping the rock into your belly, buried by both sides of my cardigan that you were wearing, holding the rock like a toy bear, and saw your eyes well up with bubbles of hot tears and your face swell like you've done since you were a baby, and that familiar sniffle that I know so well returned, and you reached into your pocket for a scrap of tissue that you used to wipe your nose, which you always do rather than blow, the rock still in one hand, wiping the other hand on your brown cords, leaving a glisten of snot like a snail's trail on the ribbed material.

Where will I put it then? you asked. I don't know, I said. There, in that bin. You can't put a rock in a bin. Anyway, I'm not leaving Rock. It's mine. Mine, mine, mine. I don't care what you say. Rock now had a name. I don't know, put it there, by the wall, that way someone else can enjoy it. What? Do you expect someone to just find it? No, I'm not leaving it. Just leave it, come on, we can't take it with us. Well, what do you want me to do? You haven't told me what you want me to do?

You always ask me that same question when my instructions are unclear, perhaps because I'm not sure myself. All I knew was that we had to go. The last thing I needed now was an argument with you, about a rock.

And then I heard it drop. It wasn't a thud or a crack, more a cushioned landing, a stone falling on grass. I looked up from hoovering, the blood returning to my body, and saw it lying on the ground next to the hoover machine, alongside an empty bag of crisps. I hadn't noticed before but sitting on the wall of the Maxol petrol station on the Swords Road, Dublin, next to the hoover, was an elderly man, just letting the world go by, oblivious to our fight. He was gaunt, almost deathly, shaving cuts on his face. He seemed lost, as if he'd walked for miles and wanted to sit down, somewhere, anywhere. The chipped breeze block wall of the garage seemed as good a place as any, as buses and lorries belched past on their way to the airport that we needed to get to. What was he doing there? He seemed like a permanent living sculpture of the garage, something that would still be there if we came back the next day. He just sat, his head staring at the rock that you had dropped by his feet, next to the hoover.

Looking at the rock that time, I could almost feel your hands leaving it, that tingle of warmth on your fingertips from gripping its edges, the sharpness cutting into your palms leaving purple blood-filled indentations.

Get in, I said, we have to go.

You wrapped my cardigan around your body and slammed the car door. I brushed some sand off the passenger seat. A knock

16

on the window. Hey, you can't leave that thing there, I heard someone shout. Jesus, who's that? I asked. Hey! Hey! The voice again. Open the window, you said. But we need to… the window whooshed open. What? I mean, yes? You can't leave that rock there, the station attendant said. Why? We can't throw it away. Sorry, we… have to go, flight to catch. But mister… I started the engine, turned my head, reversed, your hands gripping the seat. Bye, I shouted, beeped the horn and waved. We re-joined the traffic on the Swords Road. Your eyes met mine in the rear-view mirror. You always sit in the back. There was silence. Cold as ice. A taut expression on your face. Then you said, you're so embarrassing, do you know that?

*

A few days before.

I said we were going for a walk. I had to get out of the hotel. The air inside was dry, constricting. Reluctant at first, but then you dropped your headphones onto your Mac that you left open on your unmade bed, socks and t-shirts and books and used tissues scattered on the floor.

We drove. You and me out from Clifden in County Galway towards the coast. I wanted to walk on a beach. One of those beaches where even on those grey days the light seemed to go on for miles and pierce my eyes. The villages became smaller and buildings more scattered as we drove on, until the road narrowed to a lane wide enough for just one car and jungly wild ferns, fuchsias, arrow grass and wild orchids brushed against the car doors. There was moisture in the air. A salty wetness. Damp, sticky, dripping.

Where are we going? you asked. I'm looking for a beach my father took me to when I was a kid. He used to like walking there when we came here on holiday. It's somewhere around here. But we can't swim, we didn't bring any towels, you said. Well, I might dip my toes.

Thirty years on, the beach now flickered in my mind like a Super 8 film. We'd followed a handwritten sign with trá, beach in Irish, painted on it, down a lane and found a sliver of dazzling white sand, see-through water, pebbles like eyeballs, jellyfish stuck to the shore. It's where my father and I dug a ram's skull out of the sand, where we washed it, where we laughed as seawater gushed out of its eye sockets. I asked if I could take it. At first he said no one would mind, but then said that we should leave it where we found it. It was better that way, he said, better to keep things where they belong. And yet I wanted it so badly. I wanted to feel the grittiness of the sand in between my nails, snap the honeycomb bone tissue with my fingers, feel the smooth horns in my palms.

Before you and I walked, I wanted to drive across to Omey Island along the unnamed road, an expanse of sand that at low tide becomes a road of a few hundred metres. I thought it would be fun. You said that the car might get stuck in quicksand half-way, so we decided to walk. Ahead of us I could see a few rusty road signs tangled with seaweed embedded in the sand. Each one had white arrows on blue circular signs pointing forwards and backwards from either side, as if we needed reminding that whichever direction we looked, we are always going forwards and backwards.

As we walked you kept looking back at the car, wondering if we'd get back in time. I'm going back, you said. It's not safe. I can already see the tide coming in. Why is that person running? I'm cold. It's fine, I said. Look, the app says that we've got hours before we have to get back. But why is he running? He's a jogger. Come on, when do you get to walk to an island like this? I'm going back.

You shot a road sign with your phone, turned and stomped your way back across the sand, retracing your footprints, placing your shoes into the same indentation that you made on the way out, so it showed you going forwards and backwards, footprints that would soon be swept away by the tide. Ten minutes later I got to Omey Island and looked back. I could just about make you out, your black hoodie under my cardigan up over your head, a shadow against the white hire car as drizzle danced in the air. Some sun was trying to poke through the clouds but failing. You prefer it that way.

What did I expect, as I looked at you hundreds of metres away? For you to love these far-flung places on the edge of nothing? I was doing that parental thing of trying to get you to like something that you had no connection to, but I wanted you to connect to. This could be the last time I would come to this part of the world. My mother who lives in Dublin is moving to Australia soon, so I'll have less reason to come to Ireland. We used to holiday here when I was young, the sun prickling our necks on our walks before going back to a B&B, and then a meal of mussels and chips, the midges biting our bare backs as we slept. I still wanted to find the same beach nearby where we used to walk, where I found the ram's skull, where I used to skim stones with my father, where I'd curl up in a sandy towel after a dip in the icy water. I wanted to see this part of the world one last time. I wanted you to breathe it as much as I had to.

*

Empty your pockets please, an airport security guard said. Laptops in their own tray. Toiletries in a plastic bag. You emptied your pockets. One stone, then another, then another, then another. I counted sixteen: agate, basalt, conglomerate, granite, slate, rhyolite, quartzite, round, flat, oblong, pear shaped, pink, white, black, silver, blue, jade green, lime sea glass, all polished by the lick of the tide.

I thought I... What? Didn't I... You didn't say I couldn't take these. It was a pointless argument. You see. What? They didn't confiscate them. They didn't even look at them. You shoved me, your pockets now heavy again. I could have taken Rock.

But I also felt heavy, as if we'd left something behind.

*

We drove on. We were lost, trying to find the beach. Every lane we went down with handwritten signs for trá seemed all to be dead ends or driveways to empty holiday bungalows, pebbledash walls and windows reflecting the watery sky. I know you don't like not knowing where we are going, so you asked where we were going every few minutes, as if I knew. A beach, I said. I'll recognise it when I see it. For some reason though, at that moment I didn't mind that we were lost. Amidst the crisp air and lichen-stained rock, I felt that we could just drive and drive and not worry about where we'd end up and you might enjoy that. At least that is what I hoped. I wanted to tell you that sometimes my mind is a black hole and I need a rope to climb out, but getting lost felt calming, freeing. We'd eventually find the beach, a beach, any beach, somewhere where we could walk.

It was close to three that afternoon when we came across a beach near the town of Renvyle. The car was now musty with the smell of bodies, and you told me that I had promised a walk, otherwise you wouldn't have come, that you had better things to do. When I asked what those better things were, you didn't say. Come on, we're stopping here. There's a beach. Is this the one? you asked. I don't think so, but it looks beautiful.

I stepped on a length of barbed wire attached to a rickety fence with my boots so you could climb over, and we walked onto a sand dune through clumps of marram grass that scratched against our legs and down onto a beach that curved into the distance. Mackerel sky. The only sound a distant bark of a dog. The sun dead ahead of us now, still high on the horizon, lighting up our faces, glowing onto rocks that dotted the sand still wet from the tide.

You asked again if this was the beach I wanted to visit. No, I didn't think so, but it didn't matter. It was lovely anyway, and my father would probably have laid down here and let the waterlogged sand dampen his trousers and bald head, and he would have breathed.

You stopped amidst a jumble of seaweed, clumps of bulbous jelly-like roots left to dry on the sand. I looked at you from above, your eyes scrunched up behind your glasses against the sun, your hands knotted in a cat's cradle, your knees bent, and at that moment I wanted to apologise for all the things that I might not know about you, but I didn't. You just being here, with me, was enough.

I skimmed some stones, feeling the flattest ones I could find with my thumb and forefinger. They go further if they're flatter, I remember my father telling me. You tried to skim. The stones plopped into the still water in front of you. We laughed. I held your hand in mine. We both stooped forward. Our knees bent. Look into the distance, I said. Throw it like a frisbee. I can't, you said. Here, you do it. We breathed. Together. And skimmed. The first skim some feet away, the second and third in quick succession, the fourth a mere ripple into the waves. Yes, you said. I smiled. You see?

You started to gather rocks. Can I take these? you asked. Sure, I said. Are you sure it's not illegal to take rocks from a beach? I'm sure I read somewhere that it's illegal. Is it illegal? Will we be put in jail if we get caught? What? Who's going to catch us? But at the airport... Don't worry about that, I said. Why would they care? It's only a few rocks. Look, there's millions of them, millions. You smiled.

We compared stones and shells as we gathered, discarding the ones we didn't like, throwing them against other stones and pocketing the bright ones, the colourful ones, the fossils, rubbing the sand off on our trousers. It was then that you saw Rock.

It jutted up through the sand, as if it had been placed in that spot as a mark. Using your fingers you dug around the edges, sand trapping in your chipped fingernails, and pulled the rock out. White pristine quartz, with veins of earthy colours running through it like deltas of rivers, the lines on the palm of a hand. Polished and beaten by millennia of sand, seawater, wind and rain, it was perfectly smooth in places, rough in others. It somehow seemed to fit into both of your hands, large enough for you to hold, as if it wanted to be held, your hands able to mould themselves against the curves of the rock that had been blasted from something, a lost piece of glacial debris. You held it up to your ear, like a shell. What are you listening to? I asked. The sea, you said.

We washed the rock in the sea, our bare feet freezing, trousers rolled up, our bums getting wet from the lapping waves until the rock shone, translucent, a glowing white. You rubbed it dry with my cardigan and held it to your belly, not wanting to let it go, the rest of the rocks jangling in your trousers.

For a while we sat on the sand dunes and looked out. Dark rocks dotted the sea, tiny forgotten islands. The sun a whisper of light. You took out your phone and snapped.

*

You see, you said. What? I asked. I told you. What? I could have taken Rock. Here, I looked it up. There's nothing that says you can't take rocks on a plane. 34,000 feet up, this was the last conversation I wanted to have. OK, I mumbled. Sometimes I get things wrong. Sometimes. You put your earbuds back into your ears and pressed play on your mobile. I looked away. Truth be told, I'd also wanted to take Rock with us, but sometimes I don't think, and it's easier to say no to a request than say yes, as if saying yes might be more freeing and remove some kind of constriction, but I enjoy that constriction sometimes, it keeps me on edge, makes me feel that I'm in control, an edge that sometimes is hard to fall away from. So I said no. Parental choice.

*

Dublin, my mother's apartment, the day before we flew back to London. I wanted to go for a drive. I had an urge to drive along roads and see places that I hadn't been to since I was a teenager – the garage wall where I smoked dope, the park where we threw batteries into bonfires while legging it, the hotel owned by my friend's dad where he served us apple pie and vanilla ice cream in the bar like hotel guests. I had an urge to be alone, but when I told you that I was going out, you said you wanted to come as it was too early to go to bed, and you weren't a kid anymore and you also wanted to see these places and I always did things alone, so how about it?

The night was clear, t-shirt warm. I opened the windows and let the breeze tickle my face. You edged your head out of the passenger window, the air flicking your hair. Led Zep on the stereo.

In truth there wasn't much to see. An apartment block had been built on the park, the hotel was gone, the garage a Londis or some such. Why don't you stop, walk around? you asked. I ignored you for some reason. Easier to say nothing than make an excuse, like there was nowhere to park. Truth was I didn't want to stop. I had spent the last few days creating images in my mind of all these places, like the beach I'd wanted to visit, and it seemed easier for the images to stay there. They were ruined by what I'd seen, fuzzy, blurred, and I was afraid that what I'd be left with was not what I wanted to see.

We drove on. Through the suburb of Kimmage, past where the Classic Cinema had been, the old age home where my grandmother died, around Harold's Cross park, right and then left onto Leinster Road.

What are you doing? you asked. What do you mean? I said, we're going home. But, this isn't… this isn't… What? I asked, as I pulled over to the left outside number 88. This isn't your house, where Granny lives anymore, you said. I closed my eyes. I couldn't understand how it had happened. I'd driven to our old house, unconsciously, without thinking, as if I was drifting along the streets of my childhood, oblivious to what I was doing. But we are home, is what I wanted to say. I didn't. I closed the windows of the car and wanted to hide.

From the outside the house was dark, the grass in the front garden overgrown, the paint on the windowsills peeling, the lavender bed skeleton bare, the door painted red, gloss.

Come on, you said. Let's take a look. What? I asked. We can't. What if they see us? Who's they? I dunno, the new owners or something. We can't just poke about in the middle of the night. They'll think it's weird and I can't be arsed to make excuses. Yeah, do you mind us having a look? Yeah, I used to live here. No, you go. I'm not going alone. And then you grabbed my hand, and I realised that you hadn't looked for my hand like that since you were much younger. It's just not something that you do anymore, and it sent a ripple through me, as if it kind of woke me. We'll only be a sec, come on, don't be so boring.

We got out of the car and walked up the path in the front garden to the front door on our tiptoes, worried that we might wake someone. I walked over to the window of the lounge and peered inside. I felt like a thief, scouting an empty house. There wasn't much to see – a leather armchair, blank walls, a red dot on a plasma screen. Even though I was outside, I could still smell the musty carpet, see the spores of mould on the bathroom tiles, the wormed apples that lay on the ground in the back yard. What was inside now was unimportant to me, the place was still there, and at that moment, I felt like I could ring the bell and enter and re-take my place at the kitchen table or go into my old room and no one would mind.

A hall light came on. Shit, I said. Let's go, you said. We ran through the long grass, dandelions and weeds and back to the front gate. And there it was. The rock. Not the rock from the beach, another rock, but the same size, the same shape. A grey ballast rock this time, with white veins running through it. It was in exactly the same place, just as I remembered it, holding the iron gate open, like it always did, like it had done since we moved in, battered by rain and wind, blasted by sun, always there, constant, solid, still, like the old man at the garage. No one ever lifted that rock. For a while when I was a kid, my family experimented with leaving the gate closed, without the rock, letting the gate bang against the iron fence three times, but after a while the rock returned. It needed to hold the gate in place. Look, it's Rock, you said, pointing. Yes, I know. Looks the same. It's been there since we moved in. 1984. That's thirty-seven years. Where did you get it? you asked. I've no idea.

And at that moment, I wanted to pick up the rock, feel its grain against my palms, its weight strain my forearms, its roughness chip my fingernails. I realised that I'd never held that rock before and didn't have any rocks or bricks from our old house. Why is it, I asked myself, that we live in places for so long, where our skin and hair sheds, and yet we don't take anything of the building with us? The building stays, and we leave. What remains is a shell that used to house us, cocoon us, protect us.

I wanted to take Rock, to remind me of that house. At that moment it meant so much to me, as if keeping it close to me would remind me of my childhood home. My mother would soon be gone to Australia, and I'd probably never come back here, and if I held it to my ear I'd hear the sounds of the house, the classical music, the arguments, the bells from the church opposite. But I didn't. I left it holding the gate open, where it had always been. Maybe it was better that way. You crouched down and flicked your mobile on and shot, the flash filling the night sky like a beacon, blinding me. Rock, you said. Now other Rock has a friend.

*

He didn't let me take Rock, you said, the moment we walked through the front door when we got back to our home in London. What rock? my wife asked. Ahh, just some rock they found on a beach. They have plenty of other rocks; empty your pockets. I don't want to, you said. Come on, show your mother what you brought back, they're beautiful. But I wanted to have Rock, and you wouldn't let me. Why didn't you let them take this rock? my wife asked. There's no way we'd have got it through security. It was massive. You could have let them try, no? No, we were rushing. I had to get the sand out of the car, fill it up, take it back to the car rental place, which is bloody miles from the airport and we were late. I had no time for the rock. But I don't understand, why didn't you at least try? OK...

I said goodnight to you later that evening, you curled up in bed, Kindle lighting your tired eyes, my cardigan and shirts that you like to wear scattered on the floor, school uniform tossed on the back of a chair, your stones on your desk, shining under a lamp, all in a row in size order.

I enjoyed the trip, you said. Glad I came. Don't worry about Rock. I'd like to go back one day and then we can get another rock. Do you think we'll find that beach again? I'm not sure, I said. It was hard enough to find it the other day, let alone next time, if there is a next time. Let's try, you said. Maybe next summer. We can go swimming. I'll bring towels, I said.

And as I turned off your light and closed the door, I knew that I'd be lying to you if I said that we'd go back to that part of Ireland again, to those beaches, to feel that washed air fill our lungs. I didn't want to spoil the memory of that beautiful day and the stones we found, the ones we took and the ones we left behind. Even if we did go back, we'd argue about where to walk and what time the tide would come in and where we'd have lunch.

I sat on the stairs outside your room and a strain of guilt rose within me, that I'd somehow done you wrong but also done myself wrong by not taking the rock. I didn't tell you that I'd wanted to drive through Dublin alone that evening so I could discard the rock so you wouldn't have to do it, as I knew that you'd get upset, as you don't like throwing things away, but it didn't work out that way and at that moment I missed that rock as much as you did. I knew I couldn't have taken the rock from outside my old house, but the white rock, who really would have cared and why, why did I not let you take it? It was only a rock, but it was your rock, our rock, and I felt that I'd torn something from you, just as my connection to the beach, our old house, the ram's skull that was torn from me, and I wouldn't see them again. I had to get it back. I had to have it near me. I had to feel the sharpness of its edges in my palm, the sand in my fingernails. I had to see its brightness in my eyes. I had to lick the salt from its crevices. I had to hold it and smell the dripping ferns. I had to hold it to my ear and hear the sea, the rush of the wind. For you. For me.

Quickly I googled 'petrol station, Swords Road, Dublin', my fingers banging the keyboard like a hammer. There it was; the Maxol garage, a picture of the hoover machine next to the breeze block wall filling the screen of my laptop. I flicked on my phone and dialled.

*

Hi, I called earlier about a rock I was looking for. Is the manager back from his break? I asked. One moment, the voice said. It's that same fella calling… I heard the voice shout. Hello, a new voice said. Hi. Mister, we've got your rock.

Dodgy Ticker

December 2020

I'm not entirely sure when my anxiety started. Does it even matter? One day I was fine, myself, whatever that means, the next I wasn't. I realise at this moment that I'm simplifying things, but that is what it felt like, as if a switch on a fuse box had tripped inside me. Outside, I was still the same forty-five-year-old man. I'd look in the bathroom mirror and say to myself, there's nothing wrong with you, you're fine. My bald head, my trimmed beard, my out-of-control curly eyebrows all seemed the same. But inside, the threads of electricity cable controlling my nervous system had frayed. I was jumpy. Everything was heightened, tight. A tinnitus piercing rang in my ears. An acrid smell of burning filled my nostrils. My heart fluttered uncontrollably. My circuit was corrupted. I was lost.

It wasn't like things were bad, on the outside that is. What did I have to be anxious about? In September 2019 I'd left a job on my own accord that I'd been in for ten years, with a lump of cash in my back pocket. I'd no longer scoff at the posters in the lift lobby that advertised mental health support. I'd no longer get that knotted pain on the side of my forehead and breathlessness when I'd speak to certain colleagues. I'd no longer sneak in and out of the building using the fire exit through the post room by the loading bay at odd times of the day to avoid being seen. I'd no longer sink into the banquette with the furry material next to the detergent-smelling cleaners' cupboard, hidden down a corridor with flickering overhead lights, away from the crowd, to read, to write or just to play on my phone.

No, things were fine.

I'd recently finished a writing degree and was in the final stages of completing my first book. I am in a beautiful marriage and have two daughters who make me laugh and cry. Our house is an oasis of calm. Natural light floods the open-plan spaces through skylights. Our bare feet are warmed by the wooden floors heated by the sun or the underfloor heating. Tropical plants grow in abundance in the greenhouse atmosphere inside, and fill the courtyard garden outside with lush colour. We eat well. We drink well. Sometimes, we sleep well.

Was it November, or October last year? I tell myself that it doesn't matter when this all started. It's pointless celebrating an anniversary of something that no one else really knows about. But, for the purposes of this piece, it does. I need to know that it's been a year since I thought of suicide. Maybe I want to celebrate – with myself that is. Is that allowed?

And when I say frayed, I was worn out, like a threadbare towel. Outside, my eyelids flickered, my muscles did that thing when they shudder for no reason, my legs were restless. Inside, words spun hysterically in my mind: purpose, help, breath, accident, heart, why, useless, end, suicide, death, final. I never got the chance to welcome these words in. It was as if they had just been there, waiting to scuttle freely around my nervous system, to curdle my mind.

It kicked in.

Let's call my anxiety *it*. For the purposes of this. It seems apt.

And like the meaning of the word anxiety, *it* was strangling me.

So much so that *it* coursed through my body, making my heart the focus of my attention in a way I'd never thought imaginable. A constant stiff pain sat like a heavy weight behind my ribs. The weight was black, sometimes making it difficult to breathe. I'd lie in bed, I'd sit on the sofa, I'd walk our daughter to school and feel my heart pound like it was trying to escape my body, as a loop-the-loop of the words I didn't want to hear rattled in my mind. Was everything ending?

Around the same age I am now, my father picked up what he liked to call a 'dodgy ticker', as if giving it a name somehow removed his responsibility for it. It became a piece of muscle, an element of his failing, tattered system. Over the years that I grew up with him, his 'dodgy ticker' became all of our 'dodgy tickers'; my mother's, my sister's, mine. We lived with his ticker, echoing around us like a distant clock. We lived with his cardiologists: Horgan, Maguire. Tick, tick. We lived with his pills: Zocar, Aspirin, Warfarin. Tick, tick, tick. We lived with his rushed admissions to the hospital: Beaumont, St James's, Blackrock, Ballsbridge. Tick, tick, tick, tick. Until once or twice his dodgy ticker sparked, and not in a good way, but he always came home, like a machine given life with a fresh set of batteries.

I also wanted to come back from somewhere with a new set of batteries. Did I need to go some place else? Would escaping help, maybe abroad? I wasn't sure, and anyway, I couldn't go anywhere. I had commitments. But often when my wife was at work and our daughters at school, I'd lie on the floor of our study, wanting the grain of the wooden floorboards to wrap their fibres around my body, pull at me and sew me into the ground.

What was wrong with me? The more I thought about what I needed, the less I could put my finger on it. The only place my fingers went was on my pulse, gently resting the forefinger and second finger of my left hand, held together on the vein closest to the curved part of my right wrist, just like my father had shown me.

Venice, December 2003. My late twenties. Driving icy rain. Noise bursting from condensation-filled bars. Streetlights shining the saturated cobbled pavements. Smog. Upstairs in a restaurant, my father and I sat on wooden benches eating *chicchetti*, Venetian antipasti and drinking spritzes, a smell of fried fish in the air. My father had recently recovered from his latest heart operation; the installation of stents, miniscule scaffolding holding up the arteries of his 'dodgy ticker', easing the flow of blood. He told the story of the op with an almost cheery glee, a wide smile across his bristly cheeks, his eyes stretched open searching for attention. I listened, intently, the alcohol of the cocktail fizzing my head. "You're pale," he said suddenly. *Beat.* I looked away. "Look at me," he said. *Beat* "I've had this… eh… tachy… eh… cardia," I hesitated. *Beat.* He took my cold hand as if congratulating me for joining a club, and then moved his fingers to my wrist, mouthed some numbers while looking at his watch and nodded, before offering me 10mg of Valium as a straightener. *Beat.* "What are you taking?" he asked. *Beat.* "Beta-blockers." *Beat.* "Good. Keep an eye on it," he said. As if I could. I had no idea where this rapid heartbeat had come from, a beat so fast that I could barely feel the distant murmur on my wrist. Tick, tick, tick, tick, tick, tick, tick, tick, tick. Like *it*, it just appeared.

The tachycardia didn't last long, a few weeks. But I've often thought about it, as if it must have left an indelible but invisible scar on my most important muscle. I hadn't felt it since, until now that is.

November 2019 was cold, grey, still. I'd started swimming outside at the local lido, hoping the chill would regulate my ticker. After the initial shock of jumping in, the silkiness of the chlorine-infused water would numb my body. Hardly an efficient swimmer, my legs and arms would propel me through scattered leaves, lost goggles and the odd abandoned plaster, cutting through the water. For a while everything seemed clear. Often, I'd stay submerged until I could no longer feel my toes, wondering how long I could last, lost in the mist.

What was I anxious about, I repeatedly asked as I swam? I wasn't, I'd say. I WAS NOT. There's nothing wrong with you. I'm fine. Look, I can swim in the cold. There was no way I would be one of those people who go through things like this. That's for other people, over there somewhere, not here, not me. I'm strong. Look, I left my job. Strong. Look, I have money in the bank. Strong.

Sometimes I thought that I would go under and stay there, amidst the moss and plasters and leaves, and my dodgy ticker would spark like my father's, but I'd electrocute to death and the lifeguard would have to dive in and drag my sodden body to the side of the pool. Maybe they'd try to use the defibrillator. Maybe a crowd would watch. Maybe I wanted to lose myself in the mist.

No, there was nothing wrong with me.

I. Was. Fine.

Suicide.

I'd never really thought of the word suicide before. I have a friend whose brother committed suicide, and I had teenage friends who'd tried it. But I'd never come face to face with it, until now. Suicide, from the Latin sui – of oneself, from the term *fela-de-se*, or one who is guiltily concerning oneself.

Was I guiltily concerning myself? Was I even worried that all I could think of was myself?

Nothing and nobody else registered for that short time. The words, the thoughts, the cajoles, the sweet-talks, end it, end it, end it, just kept pouring into me, a sticky oily slick.

December 12th, 2019. The evening of the General Election. I'd emerged from the basement of Housmans Bookshop from my writing group into the dense haze of the Cally Road. There was the usual discussion about where to grab a drink. One or two were keen to head off to post-election wakes. I wanted to get home or get blasted. I wasn't sure. I stayed for a pint in the crowded Cally Arms, trying to make conversation among the yelps of blokes watching a Europa League match. I emptied the dregs into the back of my throat just as the exit polls lit up Broadcasting House telling us of our continuing Tory doom. My phone pulsed with text messages. I ignored them and sauntered to the bus stop, listening to Fontaines D.C. singing '*is it too real for ye?*'

Things were real, desperately real.

Earlier that day. It was a Thursday. I went as usual to The Refugee Council where I volunteer to help refugees find work. There I'd sit in an office cubicle, no natural light, and run mock interviews and help write application forms. I was doing something purposeful; I'd say to myself. Look. At. Me. And it was fulfilling. Every now and again, I'd hear that my efforts had been helpful, and someone had got a job or a place at university. I'd smile, momentarily, but was often left with a metallic taste of dissatisfaction, as if I was more concerned with myself. What about my job prospects? What was I doing? Why wasn't someone helping *me*?

That day I'd interviewed a refugee from Syria, who didn't really know what he wanted. His skills and experience in finance were strong, but he'd decided that he wanted to work in law. "Why?" I remember asking. "Why not," he replied, as if my question was perverse. "What about that job?" he'd ask as we scrolled through a website. "Oh, yeah, I could do that," he'd say. As he spoke flecks of saliva flew from his mouth and landed on my keyboard. A mist of sweat seeped through the pores of my forehead, pam pa. My heart began to pound, pam pa, pam pa. And could he not stop spitting, pam pa, pam pa, pam pa, and take my advice and concentrate on a job in finance?

After an hour he left. So did I, my headphones on, gripping my ears, my boots squelching on the sodden leaves that littered the pedestrianised street leading to Stratford train station.

The station was heaving. I stood on platform three waiting for the five past two to Wanstead Park, where I'd walk to Forest Gate, catch a connecting train to Crouch Hill and walk home. Unable to find somewhere to stand away from the crowd, I walked to the end of the platform where the front of the train usually stops. After waiting for a few minutes, my breath shallow, I realised that I hadn't touched a falafel I'd bought in the market outside the station for lunch. The silver foil heated the palm of my hand, but I was enjoying the pain. I felt the breath of people on me, their warmth rushing past, their footsteps clogging my ears, pam pa, pam pa, pam pa… conversations on phones splitting my forehead like cacophonic bells.

And as I stood gripping my falafel, the word suicide was now tattooed on my mind. I was that person. One of the twelve men who commit suicide every day. One of the men who guiltily concern themselves so much that they want it to end. Images of the artwork *Project 84* by the artist Mark Jenkins of 84 sculptures of men, their anonymous faces wrapped in scarves, manikins teetering in the wind, standing on the edges of rooftops filled my mind. I felt light as I floated above the sculptures in that silent space that lingers before something happens, a hanging air, time torn, and could see myself, now one of them, toes curled, poised at the edge, faceless to those around me.

My body would do anything now. It wasn't that I felt helpless, and writing this now I feel relieved that I can even write it down, but at the time I felt that nothing would have helped me. After all, I was helping others. Wasn't that enough? No one was helping me and even if they wanted to, they were too late.
Like the train, which was late.

I began to fret that I wouldn't get home in time to collect our daughter from her primary school. But as the thought of calling the school came to mind, I saw the five past two approach, pushing through the air. Everything slowed. The train's bullet-like shaped front gradually neared the end of the platform, as if it also wanted to come to a rest. Rest. That was what I wanted at that moment. It didn't last long. I can't tell how long, a beat? And for that beat, I didn't feel frightened. This was me. The bullet looked so inviting, so comfortable, so restful, and if I was able, somehow, to launch myself across the track without electrocuting myself and jump onto it, the bullet would mould into my body, I would curl into it, accept it, as it would accept me, and because it would all happen so slowly, there'd be no blood, and I wouldn't fall on the tracks, but instead I'd be carried away with the train, the bullet me, the bullet me, the shudders in my heart no more.

A shiver flashed through me as I watched the train come to a stop. Someone barged my shoulder. I glared at them. They didn't look around. The train did that thing when it stopped, rocked forward a bit, and then jolted back, as if it knew, like my body, that I'd gone too far and had to readjust; that feeling of hovering in mid-air, like a bird trying to fly but unable to, one claw still chained to its perch.

I realise now that I probably should have said something to someone, called my wife M, or asked a guard to bring me a cup of sugary tea. Maybe they would have helped. But I didn't, and the warmth of the carriage rushed onto me as the doors of the train whooshed open. I stood aside to let the passengers alight, entered, gripped a handrail and let the hot sauce from my falafel trickle down my trembling wrist.

Later that evening, without looking up from her phone, sitting in an armchair, M asked if I minded if she went to a friend's house to watch the grimness of the election fallout. She'd only be a couple of hours. In bed by midnight. At first I didn't look up from my mobile, as I thumbed through text after text. But I wasn't paying any attention to the election or the words around me. I was sitting on our sofa, now staring outside at the darkness that was pulling me into it, the bare plants in the garden rising like skeletons into the night, and yet in front of me was the woman I love, and I could barely look her in the eye, as if I knew that if I raised my head she'd see something she didn't want to see, a hollow, vacant me.

"No," I said, almost aggressively, "I need to..." "What?" she asked, still looking at her phone. "Can you put the phone down?" I asked. She did. I followed its trajectory to the coffee table as I started up, "I think. I think... I think I need... help." "Oh," she replied, shuffling in her chair. Truth was, I wasn't sure what I needed, anything. Just the thought of wrapping my arms around her warm back would have been enough.

I talked a bit.

She sat.

She listened.

The following morning I was in the GP surgery. I was told that

I was suffering from acute anxiety and should take something – Propranolol. I agreed and collected the prescription. We also discussed trying an antidepressant, but only after my dodgy ticker was assessed. It was paining me pretty much all the time now, leading me to believe that I would collapse or die at any moment, and M would find me dead at home or I'd die in bed. At first, I didn't take the pills.

I'd previously taken Propranolol when I'd suffered from tachycardia. They played with my body, like a joystick with a mind of its own. There was something about taking the tiny pink pills that gripped me with fear. I'd be different. I'd be a sufferer. I'd no longer be who I was or had been. I'd join that club, that club my father had been a member of for half his life. A club I never wanted to be a part of. The pills stayed in their box and this nauseous feeling of despair continued to sweep through me as the 2019 New Year approached, and we travelled to Thailand with my family for some winter sun.

It was there, after an argument with my mother on New Year's Eve, that I started taking the pills and realised that maybe I needed more than just the pills. We hadn't fought in some time, but the critical sniping became grating and I snapped, "Can you leave me alone!"

While she stormed from the restaurant, the fans spinning overhead batting mosquitos from their flightpath, I sat patiently and continued to pick at the bones from my baked sea-bream that was lathered in sticky chilli sauce and coriander, oblivious to the now muffled demands that I should "follow her and apologise… don't talk to your mother that way." Sometime later my mother and I stared at each other without saying much, goose-pimples rising on my arms in the air-conditioned lobby of the hotel. "It's not you," I said, "it's me." But really, I don't think she understood.

The new year was humid, like a wet rag on my face. The argument had dampened the evening. There were tears, and parents now glumly nursed cocktails while the children were left alone to light their Chinese lanterns. Khao Lak beach was packed. The sky twinkled with a myriad of lanterns that flew like shards of paper into the sky, some aflame, some already charred, their metal corpses plummeting into the sea, ready to choke the fish. After everyone went to sleep, I sat on the beach and lit a cigarette, my heart sprinkling a few 'welcome to 2020' palpitations through my body, a reminder that my dodgy ticker was still there, and still dodgy. The smoke of the cigarette filled my lungs and loosened me, leaving me yearning to fill my body with something, anything. The sea looked oily black and inviting, and for a brief moment I considered walking in, fully clothed, the cig sticking to my bottom lip and letting the waves swell my body with salt and water, blending with the cigarette smoke, evaporating my insides like steam, a corpse left floating with the now strangled fish… I didn't. *Beat.* I buried the embers of the cigarette stub into the sand with my big toe, took one last look at the lanterns in the sky, filling the darkness with rivulets of red, yellow, blue, walked back to the hotel, wished those by the pool a happy new year, crept into our room so I wouldn't wake the children, pulled the starched sheet over my head next to M and started to cry.

One year later.

I still take the pills and others that regulate my ticker.

It's not dodgy.

I'm still working on *it*.

Efflorescence

"You alright?" Jerry asks Ross, while fiddling with a bit of grit in the pocket of his shorts.

"Yeah," Ross says, raising his chin. "You?"

"Yeah… yeah… fine. Kids?"

"Fine, yeah. You know…" Ross pauses. "Mel?"

"She's good, yeah. The girls?"

"Doing well. School's good. Yours?"

"Still at uni. Having a great time. So I'm told… Claire?" Jerry catches Ross' eye.

Ross shrugs, looks away, and rests his arse against the curved bricks on a waist-high wall of a front garden on the pavement where they've bumped into each other; the same wall that Jerry has watched being built over the last few months, following its progress on his nightly walks.

"See they've finished the wall," Ross says, slapping the bricks.

Jerry looks at Ross quizzically. He wants to know if Ross has also been following the building of this particular wall, on this particular road. This was his walking route.

"Took them long enough… months they've been at it," Ross says.

"Looks good though, don't you think?"

"You joking me? Looks nice yeah, but black bricks? I don't think so…" Ross' belly wobbles. "They obviously haven't thought of the efflorescence."

"…efflo what?"

Ross closes his eyes and shakes his head. He does this.

"Salt deposits. Get left behind when water evaporates after the water table drops. It seeps up to the surface of the bricks. Like a stain it is. It's powdery, so you can rub it off, but it's a hard water area around here, so look," he rubs the bricks, "you can already see it coming up. Never goes away and bloody hard to get rid of if you ask me," Ross says.

"Since when did you become such a brick expert?"

Ross tilts his head, as if trying to get some water out of his ear. "I like to stay informed," he says.

Jerry smiles, not knowing what else to say. Efflorescence, he mouths a few times, rolling the word around in his mouth. He must look it up on Google when he gets home.

It's another Tuesday night. Jerry had showered. He showers every night at nine. He likes the hot water scalding his back after a day at his desk, the jump of his heart when he turns the knob to cold, the steam surrounding him. He picks at a spot between the folds of his gut. He hates his gut, his man breasts, the stretch marks on his thighs that look like those marinated anchovies. He conditions his beard and massages his face. Some radio burble is barely audible over the shower. Opening his mouth to streams of hot water, he swirls, gargles and spits.

Drying the fissured skin between his toes, Jerry can't seem to get a dream from the night before out of his head. He's never been arrested, so what did the policeman with the square shoulders and the silver stars on his lapels want from him? Those shoulders filled his frame of vision, and he can still feel a pair of handcuffs cutting into the skin on his wrists.

A shower and then a stroll. Something to look forward to. He'd started this new routine, as he likes to call it, a few months ago. Mel, his wife, thinks it's odd, and why doesn't he want to watch a boxset or something, relax, have a drink even, but he says there's nothing to watch these days, or there's too much to watch, and he can't decide what to watch, and anyway, his walks cool him down, refresh his eyes.

Today is no different. Before he leaves, he stands in the doorway to the lounge and looks at Mel from behind. She's sitting on the sofa, earbud in one ear, laptop on her knees, the sound of her nails on her keyboard, catching up on emails or whatever it is she does at this time. He rubs his neck where she nibbled him a few months ago, the sting coming back to him, and how he wasn't sure how he'd cover the teeth marks when he went to the pub, and what would he tell the lads, and would they snigger about it when he went for a piss at half-time? But then he never goes to the pub anymore. She hasn't done it since. For a moment, Jerry wants to stroke her neck like he used to in bed, or just tap her on the head. "Get off, will ye!" she'd no doubt say, so he does neither, grabs his keys and phone, and edges the front door closed behind him.

The air is tight. A warmth, like the heat from the bonnet of a car, shimmers off the road. A smell of gardens being watered. Jerry pinches his t-shirt away from his chest. His trainers rip like Sellotape on a freshly tarmacked pavement. How he'd love to skateboard down this smooth pavement, bending his knees, one arm in front, the other behind, the wind blotting the sweat on his bald head. If only he owned a skateboard. If only he could skateboard.

Jerry could, of course, get in the car and go for a drive, like he used to when the girls were young. Football, swimming, Brownies. He'd felt useful, something to do, gave him a chance to listen to the radio and catch up, so he had things to talk about, an opinion to air, stay informed. The girls are gone now, the house is quiet, the car left to get sticky from the sap of the trees. He only uses it on the weekend.

These days Jerry walks. He likes the quiet. Past the boxing club, the Shell garage, the basketball court with the torn nets, the convenience store with fruit and veg is left to shrivel outside. And it's not that he minds if he bumps into someone he knows, as he's rehearsed what to do; tilt up his chin, wave across the street, or shout a quick, "how are ye?" He is being polite after all, and wouldn't others do the same? But really, he prefers to walk alone.

Ten minutes later, Jerry crosses Topsfield Road and takes a left at Heaton Drive. It's there at the brow of the hill, where Heaton meets Clifden, where the newly finished garden wall curves around the pavement, the same wall that he's seen being built over the last few months, that he spots the distinctive figure of Ross running towards him; his dark hair matted to his head, wearing a tight sports t-shirt. As Ross approaches, Jerry's feet become heavy, and for a few seconds all his options run through his mind – say hi and continue to walk around the corner without stopping, avoid eye contact, start to run, do a speed-walking routine, point to his phone to show that he's mid-conversation. But as quickly as his thoughts enter his mind, Ross is standing in front of him, breathless, his nose dripping, sweat patches dotting his chest.

Jerry now also rests his arse on the garden wall, not too close to Ross, but close enough that he can catch a whiff of bread. He doesn't know what to say. All he can think of is that the leaves in the front yard need sweeping, and he could try and do it before he goes to bed, but by then it would be dark and the security light isn't strong enough to light the whole drive, but then again, at least he'd get it done, and that would be OK.

"Been running much?" Jerry asks.

"I can't fuckin' run anymore. I'm on the smokes again, so…" Ross says, inhaling sharply.

"Likewise."

"On the cigs?"

"No. Running. Kills my hips."

"Well, you know what they say. Back by forty, hips by fifty, knees by sixty."

"Who says that?"

"Dunno, I think I read it somewhere."

Jerry tries not to, but he can't help looking Ross up and down. He's wearing thick tracksuit bottoms. How can he run in those? A double chin furls from his neck. His forehead glistens with sweat, and his pond-like eyes look grey and misty in the light. This evening he looks different. He's bulked up, veins bulging down his biceps, pecs tight against his t-shirt, as if a new torso has been stuck onto his slim frame.

It has been some months since Jerry has seen Ross. He

knows that at some stage he'll bump into him. They only live a few roads from each other, but he doesn't picture it like this. He's heard bits and pieces about Ross and Claire from Mel; that Claire had got the house, and Ross is now living in a flat above the laundrette which is next to the bakery, and that his clothes constantly smell of bread. He gets to see the kids twice a week. Jerry had arranged to meet him for a pint after he broke up with Claire, but cancelled on him by text when Ross was already at the pub, saying he wasn't well, but really Jerry just didn't feel like it, he couldn't think of what he'd say, and ever since, he'd felt bad about it, and Mel had told him that he'd been cruel for not apologising.

"Look, I don't want to disturb your run," Jerry says, standing up.

"You're not. I need a break. This hill kills me. Every time."

Ross digs into his pocket and takes out a box of cigarettes, one of the ones with a picture of a pair of bleeding lungs. He taps the box against his other hand, pulls one out with his teeth and lights it.

"Want one?" Ross asks, his cigarette dangling from his bottom lip.

Jerry hesitates. Of course he wants one, but he knows that the smoke would make his clothes and beard smell, and Mel would notice, unless he manages to walk through the lounge and into the bathroom to brush his teeth, but then she'd ask him why he was brushing his teeth after a walk and not before bed as he usually did, and was this linked to having late night showers, and Jerry would have to make up an excuse, like he had some garlicky breath or something. He scratches the spot on his gut.

"Love one," Jerry says.

Jerry sits back down, this time closer to Ross. He taps his cigarette in tandem with Ross, letting the ash float to the ground by his feet. He doesn't speak as he smokes, as if it's a ritual that demands his undivided attention. Apart from a scooter that roars past, the only sound is the paper and tobacco sizzling in the night air.

"Fancy keying some cars?" Ross asks, flicking his cigarette stub into the air, sparks hanging in the dusk after it.

"What?" Jerry asks, now light-headed, his eyes scratchy.

"Keying a car, you know…"

"…I know what keying is."

"I saw it on this French film. Can't remember what it's called, but this father character just goes around telling really bad dad jokes and keying cars. It's not even funny. Think I saw it with Claire. Anyway, he doesn't scratch loads of cars, just one or two a day, but he takes a key between his thumb and forefinger, like this," Ross pinches his two fingers together, "and as he's walking past a Peugeot or a Renault, or one of those, he just runs the key along the body work."

"I didn't know you liked French films."

"Claire liked it. What do you say?"

"Don't be ridiculous."

"It's easy. You go on with your walk and I'll finish my run, and we'll meet in fifteen minutes."

"I'm not doing that, Mel's expecting me back."

"No she's not."

"What if someone sees me?"

"No one's going to see you. It's practically dark," Ross shakes his head again.

"You're on your own on this one." Jerry laughs a hesitant laugh, a laugh that catches in his throat, a laugh that ends with a half-smile.

"I haven't been caught, yet. Do one most evenings."

"Really?"

"I haven't done your Honda by the way, in case you were wondering."

Jerry doesn't know whether to stand or sit on the wall, so he stands and bends one foot against the wall, the sole of his trainer rubbing against the efflorescence that sprinkles on the ground, like some flour staining the pavement. His shoulders are tight, his stomach empty, his tongue sandy, the cheesy taste of the supermarket lasagne that they'd picked at for dinner in his mouth.

"Look," Ross says. "I go down Fairlight, and up Hobden, and right at Carling and up the hill, and then back past the library and back up. We'll each choose a car as we go and meet outside the school, and then we can walk back the rest of the way and compare notes. I've already spotted this Hyundai I want to do. Lovely silver thing. What do you think? It's nothing, c'mon." Ross rubs his hands together.

"Eh… you go ahead. I won't tell anyone," Jerry mumbles.

"Suit yourself."

"It's just…" There is no just. Jerry desperately tries to think of a just; that he had to finish some work, put the bins out, put the washing away, but he knows that anything he says would sound as if he was making an excuse. And now he feels bad, as

51

if he said no he'd be letting Ross down, again.

"Come on, live a little," Ross says, lightly punching Jerry on his shoulder.

"Alright," Jerry stutters, not knowing what else to say.

"Fifteen minutes?" Ross asks. "At the school, OK?"

Jerry nods.

"Right then, see ye." Ross jumps off the wall and starts running down the hill.

Jerry waits for Ross to disappear down the other side of the hill before setting off. A quick glance at his phone. Close to ten. A chill runs over his body, like when the pressure drops just before it rains. He knows the area well, but at that moment, he can't quite follow Ross' directions. Walking underneath a disused railway bridge, a fox thrashing in a flowerbed startles him; its searching eyes fixed on his. He walks on, pondering if he should just skip meeting Ross at the school and go straight home. He could always text him and tell him he'd keyed a car, but Ross was now expecting him to turn up.

The night was now pulling him in as he fiddled with the keys in his pocket. Which key would he use? The Chubb? No, that would leave too deep a scratch. His Yale house key? Too obvious, and if he dropped the key, it could be traced, if it came to that. D-lock key for his bicycle? Too circular. He chose his office drawer key. Small, sharp, useless. He could easily chuck it after he did the task. That's if he was going to do the task.

Walking up Fairlight Road, Jerry looks at every car he passes to see if it's been scratched, and runs his fingers nonchalantly along a couple of car doors to check for scratches in the paintwork. As he does, he glances over his shoulder, moving his eyes this way and that, checking for people watching him or other pedestrians who no doubt would think that he was trying to steal their car. A mist gathers on his forehead. His breath shortens. Mel would be wondering where he'd got to. He checks his phone. Nothing. What's he doing? This is ridiculous, but something gnaws at him that maybe Ross is right. Maybe he'd enjoy the feeling. Maybe he should, live a little. A tiny scratch wouldn't hurt. It would be their secret. They could compare notes. They could create a private online map and place dots on all the roads where they'd scratched cars. Every night they'd do a different car. Maybe in alphabetical order by make of car. Cars of neighbours they don't like. SUVs that take his parking place. Estate agents. Yes, estate agents' cars; those ones with their decals marketing 'your lovely new home'. Scratchers, they'd call themselves. Scratchers. Jerry takes in the cool air. OK, he thinks, just a little scratch, a quick one. He'd choose a banjaxed car, down a side street. No one would see. This would be his first.

The sky is now clear. Deathly dark. An orange hue from the streetlights on the pavements. Jerry ups his pace, feeling for the key to his office drawer, gripping the tip between his first finger and thumb, feeling the cut edges on his cuticles. There. That one. A Ford Fiesta. Silver. N-reg. Rain-stained windows. Dent on the passenger door. Loose bumper. Rusty chips on the bonnet. Torn windscreen wiper. Piles of stuff on the back seat.

Pebbledash houses down one side of Topsfield Park. TVs flicker behind drawn blinds. A distant siren wails. Jerry blinks rapidly and senses a sneeze but holds it back. The silver Ford before him, he edges towards it, the key now in his left hand, the tip of the metal glinting in the light. His breath sharp, his heart in his throat. A door slams behind him. He turns his head robotically and sees a man drop a bin liner into a wheelie bin. For a moment Jerry wants to wave at the man as if to say, *I'm not doing anything, I'm just looking around, yeah, I live close by, yeah this car belongs to a friend of mine and I'm just looking for a jumper I left in there,* but he doesn't... A dog's bark cracks the night. Quick, Jerry says under his breath. Quick. He fumbles the key in his sweaty hand. He walks purposefully along the side of the car and as he walks time slows, and for a brief moment all he can see are Ross's shoulders in his vision and the handcuffs on his skin, twisting, burning his wrists.

He inhales deeply, looks away from the car as he might when having an injection, grips the key and hears the rip of the cut along the silver paint like a knife slicing porcelain, a ribbon of metal curling at one end splintering his fingertip. Jerry stops, expecting an alarm, a shout. His heart now in his throat, he holds his breath as he runs his finger along the scar of the car, feeling the sharpness of the sliced bodywork on his skin, enjoying the edges prickling his nerve endings, just like the bite Mel gave him. He spots a shadow turn off a light in a house across the road. His feet tingle, the hairs on his arm stand up, but now there is a lightness in his legs, a clearness in his mind, a fizz in his fingers, an ease across his face. And just like that, he shuffles back to the middle of the pavement, throws the key under another car, and walks towards the school.

Ten minutes later, Jerry arrives at the school gates. No sign of Ross. He bends one foot against the gate, the efflorescence on the soles of his shoes sprinkling on the metal. He rubs his fingers together where the key indented his skin. He leans his body forward to see if Ross is running down the hill. He fumbles for his phone. Mel has texted, 'are you coming home?'

He waits.

Varifocals

It had been Mel's idea to go out for dinner.

Jerry looked across the table at her.

Sitting upright, knife and fork in either hand, he watched her mouth chew in slow motion, this way and that, her tongue swelling the flesh of her cheeks, feeling for slivers of meat and scraps of chips, her eyelids lifted, her lips stained with Merlot, her eyes looking straight at Jerry as if she was about to speak, but she didn't. Neither did Jerry. His lips were closed, his tongue glued to the bottom part of his mouth, and even though he knew that he didn't have anything to say, he couldn't speak anyway. He pressed a tongue ulcer against the crevice of his bottom teeth, feeling the sharpness of the enamel tingling the spot. Resting his chin on his hands, he knew at that moment that they'd become that couple they'd seen so many times in restaurants, cafés and pubs and had always laughed about. "Look at them, haven't said a word to each other all night," one of them would've said, but every time Jerry spotted a silent couple, it niggled him that one day, they too might become that couple, sitting opposite each other, eating, not saying a bloody word.

Mel held the menu in front of her face so Jerry could only see her forehead that shone under the lights of the restaurant. The varifocals he'd been wearing for the last six months were bothering him. "Give it a few weeks," the optician had said, but things were still blurry. He felt seasick. Moving his chin up and down to focus, Mel looked as if she was there one moment, and at the same time hazy, only partly there. She put down the menu. He lifted his chin to focus. That's better, he could see her now.

He still thought Mel was beautiful. It pissed him off that other men looked her up and down. Maybe it was the way she held herself. She exuded intelligence and calm. Her green eyes were soft, her arms strong, her walk brisk. He loved the way she always made an effort when she dressed. Tonight was no different – a pair of smart black jeans, a red belt, boots and a sharply ironed shirt. The same thing she'd worn the last time they went out.

That had been some months before. A fiftieth. Jerry didn't know them. One of Mel's work colleagues as she liked to call them, from the accountancy firm where she worked. Jerry wondered why she never called them by their names, as if naming them might force her to admit that the only friends she had were at work. Jerry spent most of the evening propped against the bar, swirling a pint and checking his phone as Mel laughed with a bunch of colleagues.

At some point a man in a leather jacket and black t-shirt came up to him and slapped him on the back. "You know," he said, his eyes swollen with beer, his breath stale, "there's more to life than checking your emails on a Saturday night." Jerry didn't know what to say. Part of him wanted to tell the man to fuck off, but he held his gaze on the man for a few seconds. There was something familiar about him; his scraggly goatee, horseshoe circles under his eyes, a bandana around his neck. "Do I know you?" Jerry asked. The man looked quizzically at Jerry. "I don't think so…" he said. "Didn't we use to work together?" Jerry asked. "I remember, at the Elephant and Castle. You were the prep-chef the night of the 232 orders. Do you remember? 232. That was some night, I'm telling you. How are you doing?" Jerry said, gulping back his beer. "Sorry to disappoint you," the man said, "I've never worked in a kitchen." "Are you sure?" "Of course I'm sure. Now stay off that phone, and enjoy yourself," he said as he pushed open the door to the bogs.

It had been Mel's idea to eat at the Elephant and Castle, the E&C. She'd mentioned it at breakfast the day before they went out, and before Jerry had a chance to speak, Mel told him that she knew that he hadn't worked there for twenty years and no, before he asked, no one would remember him, so what was there to worry about, and even if they did, wouldn't it be nice to see some former colleagues, and the food is decent, or so she'd heard as he'd never taken her there, and that's the most important thing.

"And," she said, "you might even enjoy it."

As Jerry dried his breakfast bowl, he knew that no one would remember him, and even if he did recognise someone, he had no idea what he'd say. There was no reason why he hadn't been in. Nothing had happened. He'd left on good terms. It would be nice to be noticed though. He'd feel important. They'd get special attention, a glass of wine on the house, maybe a bottle. The manager would come over. They'd shake hands. He'd introduce her to Mel. They'd make small talk about the past, who's still there and who'd moved on, the night of the 232 orders.

Jerry wanted to tell Mel about that night he cooked with Graham and Jose. That night they broke the record for serving the most customers in the history of the restaurant. But he wasn't sure if she'd be interested. How would he even start? He couldn't remember if he'd told her the story before. Maybe it's better to say nothing; he didn't want to be that person who repeats himself, who bores people. It mattered to him though.

Jerry had walked past the E&C countless times without going in. It was on his route home from work to the bus stop on Dame Street in Dublin, from the university where he worked as a librarian. He could see through the full-length windows that not much had changed, apart from the menu that now had the obligatory vegan options and a list of allergies the length of his arm. Still a wood-panelled interior, bistro chairs, waiters in black t-shirts, with a motif of an elephant standing on a table knocking over a castle, and those mini aprons that hung from the waist. Light rock playing in the background. Always 'Mercy, Mercy Me' by Robert Palmer.

And then there was the time after work one night, after he'd had a few pints with his colleagues, with the rain streaming down his face and misting his varifocals, that he sheltered under the awning of the E&C and for no reason in particular, apart from that he'd had a few jars, he pressed his nose against the glass, his breath steaming the window, and watched a table of six drench their spicy chicken wings with a blue cheese dip, their fingers stained with Tabasco, bits of celery stuck between their teeth, so he could almost smell the spice tickling his nostrils and feel the cool crunch and stringiness of the celery in between his teeth, until one of the party knocked on the window making Jerry jump and the whole table almost levitated with laughter, while another diner took a photo with their iPhone, the flash blinding Jerry, and when he'd opened his eyes one of them had pressed their nose against the window back at Jerry so he was now in eyeshot of this bearded man with brown eyes and a blood blister just below his eyelid that Jerry wanted to pick, and all Jerry could think about was that the man who was now staring at him looked like a waiter he used to work with at the E&C called Ronan, and he remembered one a night after a shift at the E&C when he sprayed Coke through a straw at Ronan's face over some order that got missed, and they ended up eye-balling each other, droplets of Coke sticking to Ronan's glasses and stubble, until they had to be separated by the manager. Jerry continued to stare at the man until he was pulled back by a friend, and all Jerry could hear was one of them say, "Fuckin' pisshead…" as they swigged back glasses of red wine to stifle their roars.

He never told Mel. He felt alone that night, just like he felt alone now.

Jerry could still feel the heat of service as they sat at a table close to the kitchen, trying to get comfortable in his waistcoat and check shirt that stretched over his gut. The spits of oil singeing the hair on his arms, the retreats into the walk-in fridges to cool down, the smokes and tea at break time, the lingering meaty smell on his chef's whites. He'd felt comfortable there. He'd had a function. Things were ordered, simple, easy to understand.

Jerry had started working there after school, moving up the ranks from deveining prawns, scouring mussels and ripping spinach, to prepping fillets of meat and fish and cooking up sauces and marinades before becoming a line chef, one of a group of three that cooked in front of a charcoal grill, frying pans hanging overhead from an extractor fan that covered them in a greasy light. Orders would fly in through the open hatch and the team would get to work, barking orders at each other, singing to whatever music was blasting from the radio, shouting for more ingredients from the prep-chefs downstairs, and sliding plates of food to the waiting staff.

"What's it going to be then?" the waitress asked. Jerry looked up at her and wondered if she recognised him. Do you recognise me? he wanted to ask. Do you know who I am? Did you know that I used to work here? Do you know that I cooked for 232 customers one night? Did you know that was the record? Did you know that I was the youngest chef employed here? He wondered if a smile would make him look younger, so he smiled and sat up straight and pushed his shoulders back and looked at her, really studied her.

"After you," Jerry said.

"No, you go," Mel said.

"You always order better than me."

"No I don't."

"Shall I give you a few more minutes?" the waitress asked.

"It's fine," Jerry said. "I'll have the horseradish burger."

"Oh, I was going to…"

"You have that, I'll choose something else."

"I'll have the rare-sliced steak."

61

"Anything to start?"

"Fancy some of those wings?" Mel asked.

"Ehhh… ok, go on then."

"Anything to drink?"

"Bottle of the house red. Is that OK with you?"

"With me?"

"Yeah."

"Jerry, you know I'm not drinking much these days."

"Since when?"

"Jesus, you never listen to…"

"But I thought, as you know…"

"What did you think?"

"As we're out like."

"I'll have a glass. Thank you."

The wings were crispy, light. Jerry and Mel took one wing at a time, almost in sequence, their fingers lightly touching as they slid the ramekin of blue cheese sauce forward and backward across the table. Jerry liked to lick the sauce off the wings, before gnawing at the flesh, letting the deep-fried meat slide down the back of his throat. Neither of them spoke as they chewed, the only sound coming from the chatter and laughter of other tables. Maybe they'd just run out of things to say. Maybe they'd said all there was to be said.

It was easy when they'd first got together, when they'd roll into each other's arms after a few drinks in the pub, sniggering at what someone was wearing or what someone had said, or some awful joke Jerry told. They were inseparable then. Eating out. Day trips. City breaks. They fucked.

But now Jerry wasn't sure what to say. He couldn't pinpoint when it had changed, but it had. These days their talk was functional, administrative. They'd talk about who was going to the shops, the chemist, the garage. They'd talk about paying bills. They'd talk about whose turn it was to visit the in-laws. But more often now they'd sit and eat, the radio burbling in the background, and watch each other chew their cereal and drink their coffee before work without saying a word, until the quiet would be broken by one of them scraping back their chair against the tiles, putting their knife and fork on the plate and sliding their dirty crockery into the dishwasher, leaving the other person alone to wipe the table down and turn the radio off, letting a different silence return. Nowadays it felt easier to say nothing. He didn't know her anymore. He didn't know what to say. Like his varifocals, things were a blur.

The toilets were just as Jerry remembered. Black tiles. Low light. Bleach smell. One of those narrow sinks that he never understood the point of, and a hand dryer that sprayed the water from his hands onto his trousers. He felt hot, so he rubbed his cheeks on the tiles, feeling the cool of the porcelain on his skin, the bristles of his beard catching on the grout, the sweat from his forehead leaving a damp mark. 'Mercy, Mercy Me' came on in the background. Jerry stopped. That song. He looked at himself in the mirror. His eyes were bloodshot, his cheeks flushed, his hair matted. Why hadn't he come back to the restaurant? What was he afraid of? Maybe returning would somehow make him feel a failure, as if he hadn't quite moved on, so he couldn't just enjoy it, like the man in the leather jacket had said. Until he returned, the restaurant, and the night of the 232 orders, would continue to be a blur. But now that he was back, he knew then that he had to tell Mel about the 232. Why wouldn't she want to hear? After all, she'd brought him here. She'd tell him he was amazing. They'd have drunken sex when they got home. They'd start talking again. Everything would be OK.

Jerry's burger was waiting for him by the time he got back to the table. As Mel cut into her rare steak, he held his burger in both hands, the bottom bun saturated with blood, horseradish sauce oozing from the sides and bit, his tongue ulcer sparking to life. The meat was tender, the pepperiness of the horseradish spicing the back of his throat. He ground black pepper over his chips and dunked them one at a time into mayo and washed it down with a glass of Merlot that saturated the pores of his mouth with a meaty richness. They didn't speak while they ate.

'*Ah, things ain't what they used to be…*'

Jerry stopped mid-chew. At that moment he wanted to swing open the door to the kitchen, slide a knife from the rack, run an apron around his waist and shout out an order. "*Where did all the blue skies go?*" he mouthed. "What did you say?" Mel asked. "Nothing, just a…" Jerry stood up, tucked his shirt into his trousers, ran his fingers around the inside waist of his pants and pulled his trousers up his hips. "Jerry," Mel said, "what are you doing?" He buttoned up his waistcoat and rolled up his shirt sleeves four times, so they were now above his elbows, took his glass of wine and knocked back the dregs, wiping his lips with the back of his hand. He put one foot on his chair. "Jerry! For fuck's sake," Mel said. "Will yeh!" But Jerry ignored her and with his other hand, stepped on to the chair, which creaked under his weight. He steadied himself and with one movement stood onto the table, his shoe crushing the remnants of the burger bun, horseradish slipping from the sides of the soles of his shoes. "*Oooohooo mercy, mercy me,*" Jerry sang while swaying his hips. "Jesus! Will you get down from there, you're making a…" Jerry looked around. "Sir! You need to get down from there," a waitress said running up to him. "Jesus! Will you look at this," another customer said. Jerry's heart was thumping. He licked his lips. He knocked a fork against his wine glass, splitting the hubbub. "Sir! I'm the manager, you need to get down from there," a man said looking up at him. "We can't have this kind of carry on…" Jerry asked the manager, "Do you recognise me?" "Excuse me?" the manager replied. "I didn't think so… ehhh… excuse me," Jerry shouted. "What?" A customer laughed. "Excuse me," Jerry said again, this time louder. "Jerry!" Mel shouted. "I, I used to, I used to work here." His chest was now heaving. "Did yeh?" a customer shouted. The rest of his table laughed. "232 orders we cooked one night. 12 March 1992." "Sir!" the manager called. "232. In one night. That's 70, every hour! I'm tellin' you. Broke the record we did. I bet no one told you that when you walked in here tonight, did they?" "Sir! I'm calling…" "Me, Randolph and Jose, in that kitchen." *Woo, mercy, mercy me…* Jerry continued to sing. He pointed his fork towards the swinging door of the kitchen. "In that kitchen." Mel gripped Jerry's leg. "Jerry," Mel was crying now, "Jerry, please, we'll be arrested." "Arrested?" Jerry said, "for what? For telling this lot what I did? What we did?" Sweat dribbled down his face, salting his eyes, his lips, pickling his skin. A slow clap started from a table, filling Jerry's ears. "Well done. Now will you get down so we can finish our dinner?" "The

65

record it was. The most this place had ever done." "What do you want?" another customer bellowed. "I want, I want… *Oh, where did all the good times go…*" he sang as he ran his hand over the sweat of his scalp, his varifocals sliding down his nose, a sinew of chicken wing still stuck between his teeth. "I want…"

"Come on down love, will yeh? I heard you. I have you. Let's go."

The Chair

Jerry sat on the toilet listening to BBC Radio 5 Live. He was holding the 'guidance for patients' leaflet on photocopied, stapled white A4 sheets of paper. That evening, Mel had told him nonchalantly that she'd found a lump in her left breast while they were watching TV on the sofa.

"So, I found a lump in my breast," she said.

"Oh," Jerry said.

"Yeah, I'm not going to worry about it, but I've made an appointment to see the Consultant. Tomorrow."

"Which one?"

"The left one."

Jerry went to go and feel it, but she shook him away.

"I just want to see what it feels like," Jerry said.

Jerry read the leaflet about breast cancer. He repeated the words he read quietly to himself. Breast, cancer, surgery, radio-therapy, diagnosis, consultation, support, charity, family. He'd taken it off the kitchen counter so the kids wouldn't see it. Mel said he could read up about it, get informed. Jerry didn't really know what that meant, but in between the anthems playing at the start of a World Cup match, he tried his best to study the leaflet.

He folded it and stuffed it into the pocket of his combat shorts, next to the other white photocopied letter he'd received that day.

The waiting room was busy the next morning. Jerry and Mel waited patiently for her appointment. She played with her mobile and Jerry sat in his grey suit, which felt a bit tight around his thighs, and looked around at the other patients waiting, mostly women. A trolley of tea and coffee was being served by two elderly volunteers in blue bibs who struggled to pick up an old metal teapot with a long spout that poured scalding water into Styrofoam cups.

"Tea, coffee?" one of the volunteers cheerily asked, manoeuvring the trolley closer to Jerry.

"No thank you," he said.

"You sure love? Looks like you need one."

"I'm fine, thank you."

Jerry looked up over his glasses at the telly. *Antiques Roadshow* was on repeat and the presenters were burbling about a porcelain vase with what looked like sea urchins stuck to the outside. Is that what a lump looks like? Jerry thought.

"Mel Ryan?" Asked an elderly consultant who was wearing a frayed blue tie tucked into his white shirt.

Mel put her long black hair into a ponytail and grabbed her puffer coat. Jerry held her hand tightly before she left, letting go at just the last second.

"Nothing to worry about," she said, and disappeared behind door number four.

Jerry knew that if the appointment was more than five minutes he'd worry. A bit like having to hold a one-nil lead for the last five minutes of a football game, he thought. If you were able to take the ball into the corner and hold it there, mess around, he liked to call it, then you'd sap the opposition's energy and territory. But that was only possible for five minutes.

Jerry hadn't told Mel about his job at the charity. The Head of Department and an HR Business Partner had called him into the windowless 'HR Confidential Room' the previous day at lunch time, when the rest of the office was quiet. They asked him to take a seat. He sat down, noticing that the soft purple cushion of the chair was warm, as if someone else had recently vacated it, and that the box of tissues on the table was empty.

They smiled at him, looking up from their laptops every few sentences. They told him that they were making cut-backs and restructures across the organisation, and his area was one that was seen as a cost efficiency, thus his role would no longer exist. As they spoke Jerry's mind began to wander, and he looked at the large screen TV bracketed onto the wall, and thought of ways he could steal it, as it was a far superior model to his telly. They gave him a document with details of his severance, his duties while on gardening leave, and information about the free confidential counselling service, should he want it. They asked if he wanted to call someone. He thought for a moment and shook his head. Jerry got up from the chair and carefully pushed it under the table.

"Jerry?" Mel said. "Jerry?"

He looked up, startled.

"I have to go for a mammogram and an MRI."

"What did he say?"

"He had a feel and thinks it's nothing, thank goodness, but

just in case, you know, they want to see inside."

Jerry pictured the consultant routinely examining his wife's left breast. He thought that he'd love to see a photo of what it looked like inside. He enjoyed looking at photos of the human body in science books and seeing how it was made up of tissue, water, blood vessels and sinew all looped together in beautiful knots.

They sat outside another room in a low-ceilinged corridor lit by humming strip lights. There was no tea or coffee or telly to watch, so Jerry ran his finger over the letter in his pocket, checked his emails and thought about how he'd tell Mel. What would they say to the kids? Who would they tell? How would he deal with it? How would he tell the lads? Would he gather them in the pub and just tell them that he'd lost his job and his wife had cancer? Would they feel sorry for him when he went for a piss at half-time and tone down their voices when he returned? Would it be the same, with her, with them, with anyone?

Mel was called into a room with a yellow radioactive sign above the door, like some nuclear reactor. A skinny woman with shoulder-length black hair walked down the corridor and sat next to Jerry.

"Mmm, excuse me, my wife is sitting there, she'll be out in a minute," Jerry said, and looked up at the woman, noticing that she was biting her raw fingernails.

"Oh," she said, "but I was told to sit here by the consultant, so I'd get noticed."

"There are some other chairs over there," Jerry said, pointing at them.

The woman didn't move for a few minutes. Jerry's foot lightly brushed her brown leather boot, so he folded his legs the other way. She sighed heavily, stood up and sat in a chair on the other side of the corridor.

Jerry thought of the chairs in the 'HR Confidential Room', and how many people must have sat on them over the past few days listening to bad news, slowly emptying the box of tissues.

"Oh, don't sit there," the first woman said to a new arrival who went to sit next to Jerry. "You don't want to sit next to that gentleman!" she said mockingly.

"There are other free chairs over there," Jerry said, "I'm holding this one for my wife. She'll be out in a minute."

"I bloody hate people like that," the first woman said loudly to her new chair neighbour while staring at him. "People who think they own the place, self-righteous twats," she continued.

Her neighbour nodded and squinted at Jerry with her small eyes and crinkly face.

The door to the reactor opened, but it was only a nurse in green overalls and a hair net. She smiled generously at those waiting as her rubber shoes squeaked along the shiny corridor. Jerry suddenly felt very alone. He couldn't get the words cancer or counselling out of his head. He wanted to feel the outside and see the inside for himself, to make sure they'd got it right, but what did he know? He'd only read the information leaflet. He was only the man with no job. All the words of the past two days poured back to him. Breast, cancer, surgery, restructure, radiotherapy, gardening, diagnosis, consultation, support, notice, charity, family, severance, counselling, confidential, chair.

A mobile phone rang. The first woman answered it.

"Hello? Look, I can't talk now... I'm having a, a check-up...

Yeah, yeah, oh the hospital. They found something. You know, a lump thingy. In my breast. Fuckin' hurts. Yeah, look I can't talk now. I'll give you a call later, alright? Alright, I'll talk to you later," she said through quiet sobs.

The door opened again and those waiting looked up. Mel sat down.

"Well?" Jerry asked.

"They don't think it's anything."

"That's good. Did they see what's inside?"

"They clamped my breast with two metal plates and took some x-rays. I have to go back upstairs. It's nothing, you can go to work now."

"No, no, I'll stay."

PART II

Doing Good

Stranger: a person who one does not know or with whom one is not familiar.

There's a stranger living in my house.

R, a twenty-eight-year-old refugee arrived in our house in north London one year ago. On arrival all he had was a tattered holdall that he left sitting against the wall outside his room. For the first few days he left his puffer coat on, the zip broken. His chunky work boots scattered rectangles of crusty mud across the floor. Every morning he'd shake my hand. It took him a few weeks to stop calling me Mister. It took me a few weeks to properly look him in the eye.

R and I received a standing ovation from our Jewish community following a presentation I gave at a meeting about the refugee crisis, and the issues facing refugees in Britain. Standing at the front of a school hall, members of the congregation offered their hands in congratulation, and patted my back before moving to a table laden with bagels, crisps and apple cake. Congregants bombarded me with questions. How did he get to the UK? What was his journey like? Was he on one of those boats you see in the news? What about the rest of his family? Why did he come? The heat from the lights and the surrounding crowd, eager to listen to my answers, made me lightheaded. We left the event early, making an excuse that one of my daughters was feeling unwell.

We found R through Refugees at Home, a charity that finds short-term accommodation for refugees and asylum seekers. My family and I wanted to do something, and despite that niggling British feeling that we were showing off by hosting a refugee, he ended up in our modern house in Crouch End, the perfect liberal middle-class accessory.

This is everything I know about R. He comes from Tehran. He has a brother, F, who is twenty-one, a fifteen-year-old sister, and a mother and father. The brothers left Iran together, travelling 2,500 kilometres by truck from Tehran across the Iranian-Turkish border to Izmir on the Aegean Sea. From there, they took an overnight boat to Thessaloniki. Yes, it was one of those small fishing boats, and yes he told me he was very scared. Once in Greece they stayed in an asylum seekers' camp. After a few weeks, the smugglers sold R a stolen Bulgarian passport. He managed to get through Greek passport control, and travelled by plane from Athens to Barcelona, and then onwards to London Gatwick, where he claimed asylum. He was taken by coach to an asylum hostel in Liverpool where he met a volunteer who helped him apply for refugee status.

R's father works in construction, his mother doesn't work, his sister goes to school. There are daily power cuts in Tehran, especially in the heat of summer. F is still stuck in Greece and every time he tries to leave on a fake passport, he is arrested and imprisoned.

R used to drive a motorcycle in Tehran and one day would like to become a Deliveroo driver in London. He only ever wanted to come to 'UK', as he calls it. He thinks 'UK' is a free country. He tells me that gay people are hanged in Iran, and if you are caught drinking alcohol, you are imprisoned for six months and given eighty lashes. He hates the Ayatollah, and does not want to go home.

Refuge: a place or situation providing safety or shelter.

R has been living in my daughter's yellow-carpeted room. She agreed to vacate her den and bunk-up with her sister. He sleeps on a single bed that has a thin mattress and a blue and white striped duvet cover and pillow. Over the past year he has meticulously peeled hundreds of *My Little Pony* stickers off the bedroom walls. The ultra-violet stars and planets that are glued to the ceiling and shine in the dark remain. The blackout blind that covers the full-length window with a sunny seaside scene of sandcastles, beach balls, seagulls, boats and starfish stays fully closed. I didn't get around to fixing the pulley cord, as if I was hiding him.

Every morning just before nine, he leaves to go to work in the pub around the corner. The manager of the pub was reluctant to take him on at first – "More trouble than it's worth, he doesn't speak a word of English." I convinced him that R was a hard worker, knowing that he needed to earn his own money and improve his English. He spends twelve hours a day washing dishes, scrubbing pots and making side orders of chips, salad and vegetables. He comes home at eleven at night, six days a week, dark rings under his eyes, quietly opening the gate and front door so as not to disturb my family and me and goes to his bed.

Sometimes, I write stories about R when he's out at work or downstairs in his room, knowing full-well that I'm exploiting his situation for my creative gain. Maybe I should stop when he's at home, but I continue, as if I want him to be in my study next to me.

Previous lodgers have come and gone. The flirtatious depressive alcoholic who got into trouble with the police, the quiet Korean traveller studying English, and the Malaysian child-psychology student, who disliked children. Having another man in the house changes things. The smell of a man is in stark contrast to my wife's and daughters'. I find myself tidying away his crusty socks that he leaves strewn around, and washing dishes left sticky in the kitchen sink overnight. Another mouth to feed, another person to manage and clean up after, an addition to the utility bills, extra responsibility.

R's few belongings take up little space in his room. There's a friendship scarf from a Europa League football match we went to last year hanging on the wall, half red for Arsenal, half blue for the forgettable Romanian side they were playing. The cavernous stadium wasn't full. Chants and songs echoed in the wind from one side to the other. The mid-week cheap ticket fans who made the effort to attend, huddled close together in heavy coats, scarves and gloves holding cups of tea, as a light snow blizzard drifted under the blazing floodlights. The match was boring, ending 6-0 to Arsenal. Some of the other fans left early, after sixty or seventy minutes, to beat the traffic. Despite my repeated suggestions to do the same, go and grab a pizza and get out of the cold, he was clear that he wanted to stay until the final whistle.

In R's room, a red folder sits on a desk I built for my daughter. Photocopied pages of A4 paper poke out, and I sometimes hear him reading phrases in English: "Please, can I have some sugar?", "Can you tell me the time, please?", "What is your name?" Orange was the first word I taught him, as we peeled oranges after dinner one evening, mouthing the word slowly, together, so he would get the pronunciation. Fruit and vegetables were helpful for colours, coins for numbers and the plants in the garden for nature. Every evening I'd gather a few new objects on the dinner table and we'd play a memory game. The first few weeks were promising. I took my time to write things down and helped him practise slowly and patiently.

R progressed quickly to different types of food, crockery and cutlery, time, colours and clothes. Simple questions and answers were soon a daily occurrence. Did he sleep well? Was he warm enough? What time was it? Was he attending his English lessons at the local college? But work got busy and the reading for my Masters piled up. I often came home late and when we did talk about his English course, he said he didn't like his teacher. His course is free, I tell myself, and I know it's hard learning a new language, but I'm frustrated that after so many lessons we can't have a conversation. If he can't even do that, how will he be able to fend for himself? After a year of lessons his grammar is non-existent, and he finds it hard to remember words. Following an instruction is not a problem, but his response is to smile, rather than speak, an air of defeat in his eyes, as if he wants me to leave him alone, for me to stop, just stop bothering him.

There is a bookcase in R's room with three shelves that I assembled on a rainy night before he arrived. On the bookcase is a tub of Fudge, a hair cream that feels like sticky wet dough. The barber around the corner I introduced R to has got to know him well. They talked about their lives in Iran as he was being shaved, snipped, and oiled. He'd return from the barbers smiling, happy that his hair looked the part. Shaved tight with a one blade on both sides and a small tuft on top, a bit curly, slightly feminine. Over the year, he lost weight and stood tall as a man of twenty-eight should. He has light stubble that he shaves every day with a Remington electric razor donated at a charity collection.

Good with his hands, I'm pleased that he helps with DIY jobs around the house and enjoys helping in the garden. He tells me that his mother also has a garden with cucumbers, peppers, tomatoes and jasmine, like ours. Skilfully he cuts the fruits at just the right point on the stem, weeds meticulously, waters the soil and brushes away the jasmine flowers that have fallen on the ground. I observe him working quietly, like a spectator, questioning if I should allow him to do this manual labour. That's not what he's here for. I let him continue as he rubs a few of the jasmine petals in his hands and breathes in their sweet summer smell while singing to himself in Farsi.

When not working, he joins us at dinner. He's happy to try the variety of food we serve – Japanese, Italian or Indian. I use Google Translate to explain what it is that we are eating. One evening he nearly choked on a roll of salmon and avocado sushi. As I banged him hard on the back, he coughed up the sushi in one long piece, the seaweed not chewed. He didn't flinch, but cried a little. Spaghetti Bolognese is his favourite. Pasta covered with rich tomato sauce and small round chunks of meat that he sprinkles with mounds of Parmesan cheese and chilli and scoops up effortlessly with a fork and spoon. When he finishes, I watch aghast as he licks his plate.

R likes to wear a t-shirt with a faded picture of Ziggy Stardust.

People I'd introduced him to asked him if he likes David Bowie. How cool, they must have thought, that a refugee would like David Bowie, the great artist who sang about spacemen, aliens and heroes in skin-tight plastic costumes and flashy makeup. His response is always the same. "Five pounds, Liverpool, asylum hostel." That usually shuts them up. His ironed Arsenal jersey and Puma hoodie that I bought for him in JD Sports hangs neatly in his wardrobe. He loves washing his clothes, finally getting to grips with using the washing machine. Realising I'm being overly critical, it irritates me that he loads it with so few items and doesn't let his clothes hang flat on the drying rack, so they end up crumpled and crusty like sodden newspaper that has been left to dry.

Host: a person who receives or entertains other people as guests.

The advice from the charity recommended doing things together. We once went swimming in the local pool. The changing cubicle smelt of chlorine and feet and we changed awkwardly, our towels wrapped around our waists, careful to not expose our naked bodies. The water was baby-bath warm and R stood at the shallow end next to the metal steps, fiddling with my spare swimming trunks that gripped tightly onto his broad waist. I beckoned him to swim alongside me, perhaps have a race, but looked away embarrassed as he immersed himself in the water as if he was in a bath, washing his underarms.

Every couple of weeks a group of my friends meet for drinks in the local pub over craft beers and stone-baked pizza. Middle-aged men out-doing each other with tales of their kids and struggles with home life and work. I often thought of inviting R and introducing him but decided against it. After handshakes, embarrassing name pronunciations that would get laughs and a few cheers, the conversation amongst my friends would settle down. I'd be left sitting quietly next to him at the end of the table, sipping our drinks and peeling slices of pizza off wooden boards, not saying much.

The annual local YMCA ten-kilometre run came around and I suggested to R that we train together and raise money for Refugees at Home. It would be a good way to get fit and for him to feel part of the community. The local paper could take a photo of a host and his refugee guest crossing the finishing line together, arm in arm, medals draped around our necks, holding aloft free sugary doughnuts. We trained once, maybe twice, pounding around the block in old tennis shoes. I ended up going on holiday the weekend of the race anyway.

R sometimes comes out with us to gatherings of hosts accompanied by their refugees. He looks well, with his new haircut, sports hoodie and Primark trainers. We gorge ourselves on food and wine. The hosts stand around talking about local politics, planning applications, Labour Party antisemitism, and school places, laughing at the preposterousness of it all, these politicians, what do they know? He stands alongside me, one hand in the pocket of his skinny jeans and the other picking his teeth with a tooth pick. I try to explain Brexit. "Come on, you must have heard of Brexit. Brexit! Don't they teach that at ESOL classes? It's historic. I think we'll end up leaving the EU, and then it will be a whole lot worse for all of us. After all, we're all immigrants," I say. The rest of the group agrees. R smiles, puts his plate down and goes to watch cartoons with my daughters on the wide-screen TV. They generously make space for him on the sofa. He laughs as Tom and Jerry chase each other into tiny holes and flinches, just slightly, when Scooby Doo jumps into the arms of Shaggy when scared.

Barclays Bank was crowded the morning we arrived to change the address of R's bank account. It should have been a simple procedure, a quick discussion with the cashier to update his contact details from the asylum seeker hostel in Liverpool to our house. The cashier looked at his refugee card and a previous bank statement, and left us waiting for the bank manager, the two of us swiping our mobiles. We were ushered into a side room and given glasses of water in plastic cups. The bank manager calmly explained that in order to change R's address, it had to be done manually. The computer system did not recognise the status of a refugee card with 'leave to remain' in the UK. It's a simple procedure but could take some time.

"Can you wait and help?" I was asked by the bank manager.

"Yes," I said, "but I need to know how long it will take. I'm expected at work."

"Not long."

R sat quietly and drew a picture of a garden with trees and flowers on a post-it note. The bank manager returned and asked for R's mobile phone number. He entered it on an iPad. It was declined. I explained to R that it had to be the same number he had when he opened the account. Again, it was declined.

"Last chance," the bank manager said. "If it fails this time, the account will be closed."

"Why did you change your mobile number?" I asked, but R just smiled, so I knew he didn't understand. There was no way I could engage with his sad and tentative smile. He continued to be a stranger to me. I would never really understand what he went through to get here and what he really thought of this, this petty bureaucracy that was blocking his right to do a simple, everyday task. I continued to be a stranger to him.

The bank manager asked again, "does he understand that this is his last chance?"

"Yes."

"Oh, old phone number," R eventually understood, scrolled through WhatsApp and punched a number into the iPad. It was accepted. I ran to catch a bus to work and left him standing outside Barclays, alone.

On the weekends when R is at home, I invite him to watch a film with us on the projector. The big screen fascinates him. He waves his hand in front of the projector to catch his shadow or make a shape of an animal with his fingers in the light. He joins us one evening towards the end of watching *Monty Python's Life of Brian*, just as Brian is being crucified and singing 'Always Look on the Bright Side of Life'. Classic British humour, I told him. My family and I sing along, dancing and holding our arms in the air pretending that we were being nailed to the cross, forgetting that R had converted to Christianity from Islam to help support his case for asylum.

Martial arts movies are his favourite, especially Jackie Chan's *Drunken Master*. He knows each fight move by heart. Perhaps it was the only film he owned at home. Like a Samurai warrior, he swings his arms confidently around the open plan lounge in front of the screen, shadow fighting, wielding swords and chains as Chan kills enemy after enemy. At the end of the film R gets down on his knees and raises his arms into the air as if he'd won the final battle. I applaud his performance. He bows at us and goes back to his room.

Like all of us he enjoys new things, the latest fashion and gadgets. I don't know why he needed a new iPhone though, spending £250 buying a refurbished model on eBay. The one he had seemed perfectly good to me. Was this really a good way of spending his hard-earned cash that he was supposed to be saving up, so he could rent his own place one day? I tried to sell his old phone but it was worthless. I put it into the recycling in the hope that someone might find it useful. Together we downloaded a variety of apps onto his new mobile to help him practise his English. Simple word searches, quizzes about time and food, card games and Harry Potter books. "No," he said, pointing at my phone, jutting his chin towards me and showing me the apps that I use to watch sport. The English speaking apps update automatically and are charged to my account, but I doubt he used them. Walking past the open door of his room most nights, I hear him watching

Iranian TV, following the exploits of Persepolis, his football team in Tehran on YouTube, or speaking to his mother or brother in Farsi, his red folder gathering dust on the bookcase.

A few weeks before R left our house, he decided that he wanted to quit working in the pub and become a security guard. His friend Mohammed had told him that the money was better, the hours more stable and the work easier. Becoming a security guard was difficult, I said, you need better English. What if something happens and you need to call the police? I couldn't imagine R sitting at the reception desk of a ghostly office block at night, watching for intruders on CCTV in a badly fitted suit, high visibility vest and cap. One night he didn't come home. The light was on and the door open. I texted him to check he was OK. "Security course," came the response. He was staying with Mohamed.

Do-gooder: a naive idealist who supports philanthropic or humanitarian causes or reforms.

The question came up over a paella and bottles of red wine in a Spanish restaurant with friends one Saturday night. I recounted the parts of R's story that I knew.

"Is that it?" someone asked. "Why are you doing this?"

I didn't know what else to say. I coughed, beads of sweat appeared on my forehead. Was I being judged? Did they think I was showing off?

"Because he needs our help, like many others do," I said, "and we have a spare room, and it's not much bother, and have you not read the newspapers and seen the homeless refugees living in tents on the streets, there's a couple in the local park, and the crisis is only getting worse, and you also have a spare bedroom, so why don't you offer your room or throw one of your kids out of their rooms and make them bunk up to give the room to a refugee?" I stopped.

The conversation paused as screens from mobile phones illuminated my friends' faces. I nibbled some of the crusty bits of rice left stuck to the sides of the paella dish and finished the dregs of my wine.

R will leave our house in a few days. I only learnt one word of Farsi this past year. Good – *Khoob*.

The Queue

Middle-aged, I was jobless and lacking direction, so I travelled to Athens to volunteer with a charity for a week, cooking for refugees. I wanted to be useful.

You collected me at Oinofyta train station, a coastal town north of Athens, and drove me to the volunteers' house, tapping a cigarette out of a slit in the window of the van. It was Sunday, everything was closed. An 80s classic played on the radio.

My bedroom was in the basement where the food was stored – cans of chickpeas, packets of spices, jars of lentils, boxes of beef tomatoes. There were bars on the window. My room smelt of onions. Condensation trickled down the walls. The tiled floor numbed my bare feet.

It was no longer day, so I made my bed and smoked out of the window. Fully clothed, I rested my head on the lumpy pillow, and tried to fall asleep in my sleeping bag. I left the door ajar and the outside light on. At some stage you switched it off. I woke in darkness, my forehead cold from a nightmare I could barely piece together. Something about chasing a young girl wearing a red jacket up a hill. Parched, I drank some water straight from the tap in the bathroom, and returned to bed, listening to the dehumidifier dripping in the background.

Friday came quickly. The air was clear, as if it had been cleaned. Feverish, I shivered despite the spring heat. I was helping, I said to myself while washing my hands that morning. Punctured with blisters, I stared at them. The lines and creases seemed more confused than usual, criss-crossing, like webs of dead ends.

A nagging sensation of uselessness knotted my stomach. For a week, I'd cooked, scoured pots, cried over onions and served the same people in the same lines waiting for the same food in Oinofyta refugee camp, knowing I could leave whenever I wanted, but they'd still be queuing long after I left.

After we cooked, you asked if I could drive, saying your head was sore from a migraine. I nodded. You threw me the keys.

My temperature rising, I drove erratically, reacting slowly to your warnings of bumps and potholes. You told me we were running late, so I accelerated, and was soon able to read the names of the trucks in front.

At some stage I asked you if the girl with the red furry coat would be there today. She'd been late every day that week, running across the football pitch, wearing trainers with no socks, just as we'd finished packing up. The day before, I'd knocked the saucepan she'd placed upside down on her head, held up two fingers and reminded her, "Two o'clock, tell mama and papa."

"She knows what time to come, they all do," you said, "we always come at the same time."

Couldn't we wait, I wanted to ask, she's just one person, who cares if she's late, but I knew we had a fixed timetable. It was a pointless discussion.

Descending from a hill, the refugee camp appeared strewn alongside the main road. Behind a cluster of cypress trees that speared into the sky, I noticed the queue was already thick.

There every day, the same pregnant woman gripped the wire fence, the flesh of her arms squeezing through the mesh, while a few children dragged sticks around her legs. I slowed onto an unfinished dirt track and watched hundreds of heads follow the van as we approached the gate.

"I'll do the talking," you said, rolling down your window.

The security guard appeared tanned from behind my sunglasses. He smoothed his oily widow's peak. You offered him a cigarette straight from the pack and lit it for him. He circled the van, knocking on the driver's window, making me jump. After a few minutes he fidgeted in his leather coat and removed a remote control. Straight-armed, he pointed it at me and laughed, his teeth chipped and yellow, and shouted something in Greek towards the security hut. The gate rattled open, just enough for the van to squeeze through.

"Drive," you said.

You pointed to the football pitch, telling me to reverse under the goal. Plastic bottles and bags lay drowned in a puddle, and above, carpets had been hung and trainers strung from the crossbar of the goalpost, sending slanted shadows onto the penalty box.

The queue magnified in the rear-view mirror as I nudged the van backwards. Lost in the enormity of the queue for a split second, my sweaty hands lost control of the steering wheel and hit the horn, emitting a roar. Together, the queue collapsed like a falling wave, hands covering heads, hats and scarves, before emerging one head at a time, gradually coming up for air.

A wind whipped the trees. Aggressive clouds swept down from the mountain. What sun was left burst through, sending streaks of light onto the two lines of the queue, one for men, one for women. Barefoot children tapped saucepans they'd placed upside down on their heads like space hats, as they danced in and out of the queue, a tempo rising from them.

I felt the eyes of the chattering mass on me as we unpacked the van in tandem. I held the table, you stretched its legs. I unlocked the back door of the van, you lifted the stainless-steel pots. I ripped open the bags of flat bread, you piled them one on top of the other. We snapped on latex gloves.

The queue teetered forward like an expectant row of dominoes, breathing as one, chests to backs. Women with chipped nails held open plastic bags and plates, some decorated with ornate flowers, others with hairline cracks. Parallel to the women the men shuffled, their heads bowed, staring into empty, tarnished saucepans and plastic bowls, as if searching for clues.

Who were these people? What were they doing here? I never asked you why you came. You never asked me.

"How many? Adult, child?" you asked, raising and lowering your hand, before holding up your fingers with the number to me.

My wrist ached from working with the uneven weight of the ladle, doling out one portion of chewy penne smothered with tomato sauce after the other. As I served, I gazed into the distance rather than into their sunken eyes, wanting to be invisible, feeling itchy having to do this.

"Watch your portion size," you said, "it's a long one today."

You scribbled numbers and notes and arrows in a notepad that was splattered with bits of food. I nodded, as if in code, and shook off some excess food. But the queue noticed, and upped their requests. Six family members became eight, two became four, a child now had a brother, a sister, an aunt.

An hour later the last pot was nearly finished. A gang of young men I hadn't seen before, sporting sharp haircuts and football shirts at the back of the queue, strutted forward. They crunched sunflower seeds in their teeth, and spat them onto the ground. One of them was skilfully flicking a football over his head onto the small of his neck, and bending forward while balancing the ball, his arms spread like a bird of prey.

"How many?" you asked the footballer, who ran his fingers through his hair.

"Six," he laughed, holding a plastic plate while squeezing the back of the neck of his friend. I caught his eye. He shook his head at me. I raised my eyebrows. He pursed his lips together.

"We only have enough for two," I said. "I need to keep some for the girl."

"She's not coming," you said, "give him what he wants so we can go."

"Two," I looked up at the man.

"Six, come on man," he said. "I have wife, boy and girl, mother and father."

"Two, that's it." I was immediately shocked at myself for

arguing with him.

You shrugged.

Using the ladle I scrapped up two portions and dolloped them onto his plate. As I did, he grasped the handle. Both of us gripping its long neck, he kept his eyes on me, and with his other hand dug out the congealed bits of food that were stuck to the edge of the ladle, and flicked them onto his plate. Still gripping, he licked each finger one at a time, before letting go of the ladle, leaving the metal handle digging into the skin of my palm.

Drops of rain dotted my waterproof jacket.

"Come on, let's go," you said, looking at the clouds. There was one portion left. You started to pack up. I grabbed a plastic container from the van. I scooped what I could into the box, the food sticking to my fingers through the ripped holes in my latex gloves, stuffing in torn scraps of bread and shreds of parsley and broken penne in tomato sauce. As I squeezed on the lid, sauce seeping from the sides, two fighter jets screamed through the air. I turned my head to follow them over the darkening hills for a few moments, following them for as long as I could.

"Duck," you shouted. I didn't react. A football struck me on the side of my head, lurching my neck sideways, as if I was being yanked like a dog by its owner. Split and shattered, my sunglasses fell to the ground, my forehead tingled electrically.

"Fuck," you said. I looked up. A cheer rose from the men who were now standing around a smoking oil drum at the other end of the football pitch. The footballer chest-pumped one of his friends, waved at me and frisbeed his empty plate against the fence.

"Go fuck yourself," I muttered in the direction of the men, and dragged hard on a cigarette you held in front of my lips.

The security guard approached, the sun reflecting into my eye from his watch face like a searchlight. He tapped his wrist. "Closing time," he grunted.

"Come on," you said.

"What about the girl?"

"Leave her."

"She said she'd be here."

"Forget about her!"

I threw you the keys to the van and ran across the pitch gripping the container of food, my boots spreading dust. Breathless, my head pounding, blood warming my eyes, I sprinted down an alley, tarpaulin-covered huts on both sides, ducking under sheets hung on lines blocking my view, coughing through the smoky smell of log fires. I ran deeper into the camp. She had to be here, somewhere. I banged on doors, not waiting for a response. Lights turned on. I shouted something. A few heads poked out. My head spun. My forehead felt like it would burst. My lungs screamed. I ran up a hill. A playground. A few kids were swinging on a tyre roped to a tree. She must be there. I'll give her the food. I'll tap the saucepan on her head. I'll have been useful.

"Get in," you shouted from the van, screeching to a stop.

I looked around. The kids had dispersed. I slammed the van door, and watched the huts disappear from view as dust blew onto the windows of the van. You turned onto the main road and went through the gears, the container of food warming my lap.

That night you left the light on as I slept. I didn't dream. I was convinced you looked in on me.

The next day you dropped me at the station. My head ached. You hummed along to an indie track I knew on the radio. The air smelled wet. I was very welcome to come again, you said. I crouched down to wave goodbye, but you sped off, the van disappearing into the Greek hills.

Meringues

The annual 'Dinner with Refugees' Christmas party, held in an opulent house in Muswell Hill was in full swing. Tinkly music played in the background, candles and cards adorned the mantelpiece, and bottles of bubbly were popped and poured into champagne flutes. Guests arrived laden with hot food wrapped in tinfoil and wore crepe paper Christmas hats that stuck to sweaty foreheads.

I was hosting R in my house, a refugee from Iran. He'd never been to a Christmas party before, so I thought we'd go along. Maybe he could make some friends.

"Which one is your refugee?" asked Patrick, introducing himself.

"You mean R?" I asked.

"Yeah, is your refugee here?" Patrick continued, licking his thin cracked lips that were stained with red wine. A cricket jumper was draped over his shoulders, and he was wearing white trousers that hung high on his waist and suede loafers with tassels. He looked anorexic, as if he'd been on an extreme diet, or was just unwell.

"He's over there," I pointed beyond a group of people who

were crowded around a circular glass table covered with food. "He's got black hair."

"They all have black hair," Patrick said.

"He's the one with the blue hoodie."

"Oh yeah. Looks like a nice lad. How long has he been with you?" Patrick asked.

"A few months."

"How's it going?"

"Good, he's quiet. All good I suppose."

"Is he good at anything?" Patrick asked.

"I'm not sure I…"

Before I could answer Patrick continued. "The lad we had was a great cook. He cooked this incredible Syrian lamb dish for us one evening when we had friends over. God, what was it called? It had chunks of braised lamb, like a soup, with yoghurt and pine nuts, spices and chickpeas. Elaine!" Patrick called over to a woman who was standing at the other side of the table, "what was the name of that lamb dish Ali made for us, do you remember?"

Elaine looked over at Patrick and me. Looking like she enjoyed her food, she was bigger than Patrick and wearing a tight-fitting silk blouse. Oval tortoise shell glasses sat on her bulbous nose, and her thinning hair bounced like it had recently been coiffed. Her face was heavily made up as if she was hiding from something. Along with everyone else, she busily filled her heavy green porcelain plate with food. Grilled slices of aubergine sprinkled with pomegranate seeds, giant couscous salad with almond flakes and roasted squash, and chicken pieces with crispy skin, raisins and sumac on a bed of rice.

"Shak… something," Elaine shouted back at Patrick, returning to her conversation. "Shakiri," she shouted again, "shakriyeh," she giggled. "I can never remember those funny names."

"Yeah, that was it, he was good at that," Patrick said.

"Come on, I'll introduce you to R," I offered.

R was sitting on a heavy plastic dining chair, the kind you find in nouveau-riche wedding venues, balancing a plate of food on his lap. He lifted a piece of crunchy bruschetta covered in roasted cherry tomatoes, garlic and basil to his mouth which snapped when he bit into it, the topping collapsing onto his plate.

"R," I said, interrupting his food, "meet Patrick."

Still chewing, R stood up, holding his plate of food with one hand and shook Patrick's hand with the other.

"Hi, what is your name?" R asked slowly.

"Patrick."

"Pat-rick," R said, rolling the r.

"Yes, it's Patrick, it's an Irish name," he said impatiently.

"Patrick also has a refugee living with him," I said to R, who simply smiled.

"Well, actually, we don't anymore. At least not right now, but don't tell him," Patrick interrupted.

"So, what are you doing here?" I asked.

"The food, there's always good food at these events," he laughed. "Oh, and the company, something to do I suppose. It's Christmas," he paused. "Yeah, let's just say it didn't work out. The lad left after a couple of months, saying that he was moving in with a friend. One dinner party too many maybe. I invited him tonight actually, thought he'd like to make his shakiri."

"Shakriyeh," I corrected him.

"Yeah, shakriyeh… and so that he could meet some of the others."

"Is he here?" I asked.

"Not yet, he might turn up later."

R sat back down next to another refugee. They both looked straight ahead and poked at their food, trying their best not to make eye contact, as if on a first date that wasn't going well. Same age, probably the same journey to the UK, the silence between them seemed like an empty diary – lots to say but no idea where and how to start.

R and I joined a few couples who were grouped together trying to talk and eat while balancing wine glasses on their plates. As we nibbled, the conversation drifted in and out of local news and politics, planning applications and school places. R stood straight and stiff amongst us, hands in the pockets of his skinny jeans, nodding politely. I tried to explain some of the conversation to him, the intricacies of school catchment areas, laughing at the ridiculousness of it all.

"It all depends on where they measure the catchment area from, you see. The headmaster's desk or the school gates. I don't know which one it is, but either way it's a joke that we have to go through this. And the stress for the families and kids, especially those who move," I insisted. Everyone nodded in agreement.

R smiled his tentative smile. His dark hair was shaved on both sides, leaving a few short curls on top, and his face looked flushed from the wine and heat of the bright spotlights that shone from the ceiling of the architect-designed kitchen extension. Walking stiffly, he shuffled as if it was painful for him to bend his knees. He'd had a chest infection for some weeks and started to cough abruptly, so I banged his back a few times, tears welling up in his eyes.

"Have you seen Elaine's meringues?" Patrick yelped with excitement.

In the centre of the table was a circular mirror serving unit that reflected the ceiling spotlights and rotated gently on a motor, like in a Chinese restaurant. On a silver serving platter sat a tower of plump white and pink meringues, swirls and swishes of perfectly cushioned pristine baked egg white, one piled gently on the other like an untouched snowy alpine scene.

Waterfalls of chocolate and strawberry sauces trickled through the crevices that had cracked slightly into the meringues, creating a river of sauce on clumps of raspberries that surrounded the bottom of the pile. No one had yet dared to spoil the immaculate presentation.

"Elaine's party piece," Patrick announced. "She's won prizes for her meringues, you know," he said proudly. "First at the Church of St John annual baking competition, three years running."

"They look sensational, what's your secret?" I asked.

"They are," Elaine said, now standing next to me. Her breath smelt of wine and bits of parsley were stuck between her teeth.

"It's all in the beating you know, and the timing," she continued. "Never, never open the oven. Keep it closed tight and don't even look to see what's happening. I'm awfully superstitious that way. Sometimes I hide in the bathroom or the garden when they're cooking, so I don't tempt myself to look. One time Patrick opened the oven to have a peek, unable to control himself. Ruined. The whole lot. Ruined."

"Shall we try one?" Patrick asked, jumping in.

"Maybe one of the, you know, boys, should go first," Elaine said.

"You mean refugees," I said.

"Yes," Elaine studied me through her glasses that were thick as magnifying lenses, covering her melon-shaped face.

R went first. I knew he had a sweet tooth. The crowd hushed in anticipation, now circling the table like an audience watching a spectacle. The music was turned down. I scrunched up my Christmas hat. Elaine passed R a pair of silver tongs that had 'Elaine Dixon, Baker Supreme, 2013, 2014, 2015' engraved on one side.

"Please, take whichever one you want," she motioned to R, holding his arm gently, "and don't forget the cream and raspberries." She smiled and clapped her hands lightly like an over-excited child.

R ran the tongs up and down the snowy range, carefully eyeing up his choice, a wide anticipation in his eyes. The small meringues with tiny chocolate-coated tips sat at the top of the pile while the heavier ones supported the peaked structure. R went large and pincered a crispy thick meringue the size of a grapefruit on the bottom layer. He slowly pulled and pinched two of the baked wonders with the tongs, one at a time, like he was extracting milk teeth. Edging them out carefully, they made a light raspy sound as they rubbed against the others. He placed the meringues slowly onto his china plate, scooped up some whipped cream and fresh raspberries and dug in. The crowd breathed and returned to their plates of food, the main event over. A toothy smile swept over Elaine's face.

R passed me the tongs. I went in for my helping and dug deep into the hole that R had made, searching for the thickest, juiciest, stickiest meringue. My hand was deep in the cave when the avalanche began. At first, a few sticky drops of sugary syrup dripped onto my wrist, but as I removed my hand and the tongs, the mountain range collapsed into itself like a volcanic crater. Peaks and edges broke off, collapsing into soggy piles of chewy sugar into a casserole, and cracks of white crumbliness fell away like snowdrift onto cheese boards and into wine glasses. The chocolate-covered peaks crashed onto plates and cutlery, and strawberry sauce cascaded onto the table, and started to drip, one drop of syrupy sauce at a time, onto the oak floor.

"I'm so sorry," I said turning to Elaine.

"Patrick!" she cried, "Patrick, it's been ruined."

"It's OK darling, come on, let's go," Patrick said.

"Look, stay," I pleaded, "it's been a lovely evening. We can salvage them." I started to put the broken shells of loveliness back together while trying to avoid crushing more chunks of splendour that had fallen onto the floor.

"My meringues," she said, looking up at me. "They were meant to be a treat, not for you, for them," she barked. "I wanted the boys to enjoy them. After all they've been through. I just wanted to do something nice, for them." She was sobbing and tears had filled her lenses like petri dishes. The guests parted as Patrick and Elaine walked out of the kitchen.

I went to sit next to R who was enjoying digging into the crunchy mess and picking his teeth to remove the chewy bits. Next to me was another refugee dressed in black jeans and a tight black t-shirt. He told me that he was a qualified karate instructor, but was now training to be a hairdresser. R and the karate instructor exchanged a few words in Farsi before slumping back into their plastic chairs.

A new refugee arrived carrying a white oval dish covered in tinfoil.

"What did you bring?" I asked.

"Shakriyeh," he responded.

The Mess

There's something about cleaning up other people's mess.

It's the end of my shift in the café. I spray and wipe the tables with disinfectant, lift the chairs onto them, and sweep up the droppings that customers have left, offerings stuck to the ground for me to dispose of. The arts centre attracts these types. Liberal parents who couldn't care less if their kids run riot flicking babyccinos and pastries at each other, disturbing customers reading the Sunday papers, eating brunch and sipping flat whites.

I hadn't seen M in three weeks. She'd been picking olives with farmers in the Palestinian West Bank. We'd only had a few intermittent and disturbed conversations on crackly WhatsApp calls. She mentioned she was going over dinner one evening.

"I'm going to pick olives with Palestinian farmers in the West Bank," she said nonchalantly.

"Oh," I responded, "when?"

"In a few weeks."

"So soon?"

"Why not?"

"Why didn't you tell me?"

"I am telling you."

"But it's, like, dangerous. You sure it's a good idea?"

"I'll be fine. I have to do something."

"There's not going to be any of that human shield stuff, is there?"

"No, we're going to pick olives, with farmers, help them get their crop in before their fields are burnt to the ground. Don't worry," she smiled hesitatingly.

I gather up the unsold chocolate brownies into a brown paper bag, lock the doors of the café and cycle to M's flat off the Holloway Road. It's late October and the night air is foggy and smoky, as if an industrial bonfire is burning over the city. Fireworks crackle and explode above me as I cycle, making me jump. The road is wet and the markings greasy with the residue of petrol dripping from car exhausts. Take-away shopfronts light up the road and steamy condensation covers up the inside of their windows.

M lives a few roads away from the traffic, but the hum is constant. Her narrow maisonette is more stairs than apartment, with oddly shaped rooms off various landings. A tight pine double bed has been squeezed into her bedroom where we can just about lie side by side.

M's face, usually fresh and alive, has been singed by the sun. Her curly blonde hair is tied up with a scraggly hairband, her eyes bloodshot. I spot lines on her forehead I'd never seen before, and there's a hesitation in her smile. We hug, awkwardly bending our chests towards each other and kiss lightly.

I give her the bag of brownies, and we sit silently nibbling and sipping tea. I'm hungry after a long shift but eat slowly, following her pace. We look deeply into each other's eyes for as long as we can take it.

"So," I start.

"No," she says quickly, "what have you been up to?"

"Not much to tell. The hungry masses of Hampstead keep on coming."

"Busy then?"

"Sure, it's been busy," I say as I bite into a hazelnut lost in the rich flesh of the brownie, "but I can't get over the mess people leave. One family, they come in all the time. They wave at me as if I'm a servant, even though they know well and good that we don't do table service. And because I'm nice and helpful, I go over with a menu, and it's always the same. I'll have this, and she'll have that, and the kids will have this. And so many off-menu orders – tuna with no cucumber, eggs with no avocado, tahini dressing with no this and that. Who the hell doesn't like cucumber? And so, we make it, and they eat and pay and leave a nice tip, but the fucking mess. Torn pitta and blobs of mayo and bits of yolk and carrots that they've stuffed into their kids' gobby mouths and coffee and hot chocolates spilt, left sticky and matted to piles of tissue on the table. It's a fucking car crash. And then, they just leave. And guess who gets to clean it up?"

"Sounds fun," M responds, picking bits of chocolate from her teeth.

Her grey and red rucksack that she's travelled the world with, like an old friend moulded to her, sits against the wall next to the door of her bedroom. She digs deep into it and brings out a gift, wrapped in a thick walking sock with a ribbon tied around it.

"That's all I could get," she says, handing it over.

It's a tall thin jug made of Hebron blue glass. Its spout and handle is curved beautifully, lifting the piece like a swan. I look at M through one of the bigger bubbles that act as magnifying glasses, and watch her face blend into the blueness as if she's diving into deep blue water.

"It's original," M says, "made by craftspeople who've been doing the same thing for hundreds of years. Their factory gets raided regularly. They destroy their goods, machines, their produce. That's all they have." A faint tone of anger rises in her as I run my finger down the jug, feeling the softness and attention given to it by the craftsman.

We have sex quietly and lie next to each other, looking up at the bare white ceiling of her bedroom.

"So," I try again, as we share a Camel Blue, like teenagers passing a spliff.

"Not yet," she insists, an embarrassed pause in her speech.

I had asked M to text me photos of her trip. To begin with, they arrived daily, group shots of volunteers picking olives and eating under ancient trees on rocky dry farmland. A few days later a picture of the group, now wearing keffiyehs, talking to officials with serious faces under a portrait of Yasser Arafat. After that, there was nothing, for a week, not even a text. I called and called and texted and called. No response, until one afternoon M answered saying she couldn't talk. They were going on a protest to protect the village well from being blown up. All I could hear was the sound of boots on a rocky path and chanting in Arabic, and then she had to go, and there was no time to talk, and she was fine. Bye. Why hadn't she called or texted, had she lost interest, was she prioritising?

"Did you get to the protest at the well?" I ask.

"Not yet, please," M insists.

"But when?" I say. "I was worried about you. You didn't return my calls."

"No, they stopped us," she sighs.

"Who?"

"The army."

"Was anyone hurt, did you get hurt?"

"No one was hurt, I'm not hurt," M says, taking another cigarette.

"Is that it?" I ask. "Were any shots fired? What happened?" I shake her gently.

"Nothing happened," she says, shrugging me off. "We couldn't get through. They blew up the well. The bricks just flew, flew into the air," she lifts her hands, "whoosh. You working tomorrow?" M asks.

"Yep, more cappuccino making for me."

"Why don't you ask that family to leave if they behave so badly?"

"It's not that bad."

"Well, tell them to clean up their own mess, you owe it to yourself."

"I owe it to myself? What do you want me to do? I can't throw them out; they're paying customers."

"Of course you can," M continues, "you just don't want to."

I owe it to myself, I repeat in my head. I owe it to myself to do what? All of a sudden my cleaning up after the middle classes of north London doesn't seem good enough. I get up, wrap a towel around my waist and go to shower. The water is scalding, and the steam quickly sticks to the plastic shower curtain like a thick mist and covers the mirror. The soap feels good on my hands that are blistered from the steam arm of the coffee machine and the dishwasher. M joins me, stepping carefully into the ceramic bath that's filling with water and buries her head into my chest.

I arrive at the café the next day for my shift. A fresh batch of chocolate brownies has been delivered. I charge the coffee machine for my first cappuccino, always for the car salesman from the showroom across the road.

"What's the special?" he asks.

"Spinach lasagne," I respond.

"Great, I'll be back," he says, pointing at me. I spot M behind him in the queue wearing her rucksack.

"Going somewhere?" I ask.

"I thought I'd have a brownie and a coffee before I go," M responds.

"Where?" I ask.

"To help clean up the mess."

Persepolis

The trousers of Jerry's M&S woollen suit, that he hadn't worn since he'd taken redundancy a few months earlier, felt tight against his thighs. Worried that he'd rip a hole in the seat if he bent over too quickly, he knelt on the pavement to lock his motorcycle, the rust of the wet chain staining his fingers. He had forgotten to ask Fatima, the volunteer manager, about the dress code, but thought that as he was putting his twenty years of experience as a recruitment consultant to good use, helping refugees find work, he should dress smartly. Anyway, Mel, his wife, had told him that he looked very professional as she tidied his tie before he'd left home that morning. Jerry felt good as he drove off, pleased that he still impressed her.

As Jerry pressed the buzzer of the Waterloo Refugee Network, he looked around at the Old Vic theatre behind him. *Endgame* by Samuel Beckett was still playing. He'd seen it some weeks earlier with an arty friend from university and pretended to understand it. When Mel had asked him in bed that night what he'd thought, he said, "I'm not sure. I just thought it was very cruel, you know. All that climbing up ladders that Clov the servant character does, constantly trying to leave. Must be exhausting, especially when he knows he can't leave. I don't know why Evan found it so funny." Mel nodded, her lips closed, and returned to her book.

"I'm here to see Fatima," Jerry spoke into the intercom, noticing his breath smelling of coffee.

"Who?" a crackly voice asked.

"Fatima?"

"She isn't here today."

"Oh, I'm sure she told me to start today."

"Are you making a delivery?"

"Can I come in, please?"

Jerry pushed on the glass door and waited. A few seconds later the door buzzed and unlocked, and he entered a brightly lit reception area that looked like a stark doctor's surgery.

"Hi, I'm eh, starting, today. As a volunteer. My name's Jerry. Jerry Ryan," he said to the receptionist, as a gust of hot air from an overhead heater warmed the bald patch on his head.

"Please wait," she said, pointing him to the waiting area.

Jerry sat on the only free plastic seat, and bent his head forwards so he could listen to the receptionist as she spoke into a telephone. "There's a man here, for Fatima… I know… I told him that she isn't here. What shall I say to him?" After a minute she looked up at Jerry. "Someone's coming."

"Look, I don't know what Fatima told you, but we're really busy today. Have you seen all these people? It's really not a good day to start. I don't know where they've all come from. You just never know with the bloody Home Office and their systems and processes and paperwork," Larry, another volunteer manager said as they walked through the low-ceilinged windowless office. Jerry only half-listened, instead focusing his eyes on the silver tongue stud that jiggled inside Larry's mouth as he spoke. Why would someone do that to themselves, Jerry wanted to know, and didn't it get in the way when he ate?

"They don't deal with anyone for months, sometimes years," Larry continued, "and then all of a sudden they process a whole load at once. It's like buses. Most of these people are still on the streets, mind you, and now they're all looking for work, which is a good thing I suppose. What did you say your name was?"

"Jerry. My mates call me Jer or Jero, but my wife calls me Jeremiah. I don't mind," he chuckled.

"I'm eh, Larry," he smiled. They shook hands.

"Well I'm here now. Got full marks in the online training course, you know."

"What? OK, eh, give me five minutes. You can see some of my appointments. I'll get you some paperwork and you'll be able to start. Sit here," Larry pointed to a cubicle with two chairs, a desk and a PC, "and help yourself to tea and coffee," he shouted as he walked away.

A shot of static electricity fizzed Jerry's fingers as he took off his suit jacket and hung it on the back of the cushioned chair. He rolled up his shirt sleeves and arranged his green, red, black and blue pens in his shirt pocket. Careful not to stretch his trousers, he crouched under the desk, his belly hanging over his belt, pressing against the fabric of his white shirt, and turned on the PC. It wasn't yet lunchtime, but the office smelt of melted cheesy food, and some left-over chocolate birthday cake lay crumbling on a paper plate on top of a filing cabinet. Jerry was tempted to

113

grab the end piece which had a cocktail umbrella stuck into it, but decided not to. Maybe one of the refugees might want it.

"Here. This should keep you busy," Larry said, handing Jerry a pile of files. "Remember, don't give them your personal details. No phone numbers, no emails and definitely don't invite them around for dinner or anything like that, or offer to help outside of work, or give them any money. Help with their CVs, application letters, competency-based interview questions, that kind of stuff. Keep a record of what you've done on these sheets, give them their fiver for travel expenses, and get them to sign here," he said, pointing to a record book. "That's it. Simple. OK?"

"Got it."

"Call me if you need anything." Jerry nodded, but Larry had already wandered off.

For the next few hours before lunch, Jerry was in his element. He saw three refugees, edited their CVs and re-wrote application letters and gave advice on interview techniques, passing on Jerry's 'signature interview tricks', as he liked to call them. He'd taught himself these over the years, and was told by interviewees that they never failed. How a candidate should always pause, just for a second or two before answering a question. How to shake a hand really well, by being firm and not gripping the other person's fingers while looking the recruiter straight in the eye to show you mean business, and how to never tell the truth when asked about strengths and weaknesses. Jerry had a high-achieving percentage score of getting people into work. He was told so at his last appraisal, getting 'positive performance' and a decent bonus. But a few months later, it was suggested to him that because of his age, now would be a good time to take up the offer of redundancy and leave. He did so reluctantly, never really understanding why.

Jerry ripped the plastic cover from the package of his Greggs coronation chicken sandwich as he sat on a bench in Waterloo Millennium Green during his lunch hour, autumn leaves swirling by his feet. He threw the crusts to a couple of pigeons that gathered close by, and looked over at the Old Vic. Maybe he should see *Endgame* again, he thought. Maybe he should take Mel and ask her what she made of it. Maybe she could explain it to him, but he knew that she hated going to the theatre. "I don't like having to watch people act," he could hear her say. "It's so cringey, it's not real life."

Jerry was checking WhatsApp on his mobile after lunch when his next appointment arrived. A young man slumped down onto the spare chair in the cubicle, a waft of strong deodorant rising from him. Jerry stood up and held out his hand. Still sitting, the man shook it limply, which confused Jerry, as he noticed a vein running along the top of his biceps that bulged the sleeves of his tight Adidas t-shirt. Possibly in his early twenties, he wasn't wearing a jacket, despite the outside chill, and his jeans were ripped at the knee. Some light stubble covered his moustache, giving him a boyish look, and a clump of thicker hairs was growing around a scar that ran down one of his cheeks. He smiled at Jerry, a hesitant smile, as if he'd he just been told a joke that he didn't get.

"Hi," Jerry said, "my name is Jerry." He spoke slowly. "I'm a volunteer. I help people like you find work. What's your name?"

"Azad," he said softly.

"Larry gave me your file." Jerry opened up the folder and started to leaf through some print-outs. "It says here," he ran his finger under the words, "that you want to find work with a football club, is that right?"

Azad shrugged.

"What experience do you have?"

"Coach."

"Oh, great, who do you support then? Chelsea? Man United? Arsenal?"

Azad shook his head. "Persepolis."

"Pardon?"

"Persepolis, in Tehran." He took out a Huawei mobile from his trouser pocket, and flicked through some photos of footballers in red shirts. "You know this one? Saunders… you know?" he asked, holding up the cracked screen to Jerry.

"Who?"

"Saunders, you know, footballer." He struggled to pronounce his name.

"Oh… Irish lad, didn't he play for Celtic some years ago?" Jerry said, trying to show off his football knowledge.

"Good player. Striker. Now he plays for Persepolis."

Jerry thought it strange that a journeyman footballer like Tony Saunders, who Jerry remembered reading had moved from club to club, unable to find success or settle, was now playing in Iran and was Azad's favourite player.

"So, tell me about your experience. Did you bring your CV?"

Azad didn't respond, but edged his chair closer to Jerry's, so that the metal frames of the chairs were touching. He pressed the home button on his phone. Jerry moved his eyes so he could get a closer look, and saw the display fill up with a picture of Azad with his arm around another man's shoulder. They were standing on what looked like a jetty, the sun beaming behind them. The other man was taller than Azad and older too. He had a neatly trimmed beard and a cropped haircut, shaved on both sides and thicker on top. His back bent, he was leaning on Azad for support, and was carrying a hold-all with his other arm.

"My brother," Azad said, raising his chin at Jerry.

"Oh."

"He's in Greece."

"Whereabouts?"

"Thessaloniki. Can you help?"

"I'm not sure I..."

"Three years he is staying in Greece," Azad interrupted. "I come to UK, but he still in Greece. Twenty-five times he tries to get out."

"Twenty-five?" Jerry said incredulously. "How?"

Azad laughed, which Jerry didn't understand. Was this a joke? Was there a punch line he missed, like when the audience started laughing at nothing in *Endgame*?

"When did you last see him?" Jerry asked.

"I send him money. Before I come to London I work on a farm, you know, strawberries and potatoes and carrots. Can you help?"

"Yes. Why don't we start with your CV? I'm sure there are plenty of jobs in football you can apply for. Have you looked at working in a stadium? You know, selling drinks or programmes or..."

"No… you, you go to Greece, and help my brother at the airport, and bring him to UK," he said in a hushed tone.

"What? I can't do that?"

"Why not? My other friend, she try."

"And what happened to her?"

"She came back to UK, he stay in Greece."

"Well then." Jerry sat up in his chair and straightened his tie. "Anyway, I'm not her. Now, shall we go over your CV?"

"Please. He's going crazy in Greece, please…"

Was this some kind of joke? No, Jerry couldn't help, even though the idea of maybe driving back across Europe rather than flying, with Azad's brother on the floor of the back seat with a blanket over him, the sun beaming into his car, stopping at seaside towns to eat fresh fish and drink cold white wine appealed to him, and sure they never check the car when he goes over on the ferry on his annual booze cruise to France and he doesn't have a job, so… No, how would he explain it to Mel? Oh, Mel love, I'm just popping over to Greece for a few days to help this refugee's brother get out. He's been there for three years. Yeah, I only just met him, but I'm sure it's legit. Of course I trust him. Sure why not? It's the least I can do. People do this stuff all the time, don't they? "Would you listen to yourself, Jerry," Mel would say. Who was he fooling? She'd never go for it. Anyway, he had to save his redundancy package, and didn't have any money to travel. No. He had to say no.

"I'm sorry. No…" Jerry shuffled his chair away from Azad. "I can't, it's not safe."

Azad laughed. "Safe? It's safe for you."

Jerry paused and ran his fingers under his tight shirt collar.

"Now, where were we?" Jerry asked. He turned the ball on his mouse, and started to type, 'jobs in football stadiums' into Google.

"You, Jerry, think about it," Azad lightly punched Jerry on the shoulder, making him wince. "See you. I come back next week." He grabbed the fiver, slipped his mobile into his pocket and stood up. As Jerry watched him walk away, re-runs of Clov climbing up the ladder to the window of his cell in *Endgame* came into his mind, up and down, climbing towards the window, moving the ladder every few minutes to get a peek of the outside world, desperately trying to get out.

PART III

Number One Ennis Road

27 May 2019, Limerick, Ireland

4.00 pm

Condensation trickled down inside the window of the Bus Éireann coach as it turned into Limerick Bus Station. Before my mother and I alighted, I took one last look at page nine of chapter one from the manuscript of my father's unfinished memoir, *Dream On*, and read… *1939. Aged 6, a horse appeared one dark night at the back window of our new house in Limerick, 1 Ennis Road, the last one we lived in before we moved to Dublin. I loved that house…*

I knew I wouldn't find number one Ennis Road. The week before, a maps curator at the British Library had unfurled road maps of the city of Limerick dating from the present day back to the early 1900s. As I stared down at the unfamiliar streets, I noticed that none of the houses on Ennis Road or the surrounding streets had numbers and wondered how we'd ever find it.

My father had died a few years before, but always spoke fondly of his early childhood in Limerick. It was a part of his life I knew little about, so I thought we should try and look for this house, the house with the horse, the house he seemingly loved. I had no idea what I was hoping to find.

4.45 pm

The taxi pulled up outside a pebbledash house that looked like any other 1970s semi. A red-brick arch curved over the porch of the front door. Dull-grey afternoon light reflected against the front windows. Cherry blossom had blown into the cracks of the paving stones in the bare front garden. A Volvo estate was parked in the driveway, its lights still on, as if the driver was expecting to only be inside for a few minutes. My mother said she'd prefer to wait by the gate.

The doorbell chimed. It was cold for late May, so I stuffed my hands into the pockets of my jeans. Drizzle sprinkled in the air.

"One moment," I heard someone call. Feet stomped. A chain rattled. A key turned.

"Are you here to collect him now?" a woman's voice shouted before I could see her. The door opened ajar, releasing a waft of cauliflower, or was it fish? A woman dressed as a nurse in white trousers, shoes and a polo shirt stood in the doorway.

"Hi," I said, "is this," I coughed, "…is this number one Ennis Road?"

"So you're not from the hospice then, are you?" she asked, her feet tapping the plastic door mat. "They said they'd collect him at half past, and it's well after now." She looked beyond me towards the driveway and up to the sky. "I'm after giving him his tea. What was it you wanted?"

"Is this number one Ennis…"

"…sure I can never remember what this house is called," she interrupted.

She swung the door wide open so I could now see to the end of the hallway. There, in another room at the back of the house, an elderly man sat at the head of a table. Wearing a dressing gown, his back was bent over a steaming bowl of food. As he raised a spoon to his lips he slurped loudly, as if he was inhaling hot soup. Every few slurps, like my father used to do, he removed a handkerchief from his pocket and wiped his mouth.

The nurse rushed towards the man and spoke loudly in his ear, "Mr McCarthy, what's the name of this house?"

He turned his head, and whispered something to the nurse.

"Cairn House," the nurse shouted back at me.

"Does the house have a number?" I asked.

"Not as far as I know, and God help him, he doesn't have a clue either," she said, rolling her eyes at me as she walked back to the front door.

"It's just…" I swiped my phone on and opened the photo app. "It's meant to be here." I lifted the phone to her face, showing her a photo of a map I'd taken in the library, pinpointing where the curator thought number one Ennis Road could be.

"Look, I'm not from around here, why don't you try Osborne's Pharmacy around the corner. All the local knowledge is in that place."

"Can you ask him if he knows if any Jewish families lived here?"

"There haven't been any of that lot in Limerick for a while now," she said hurriedly, "and sure, he doesn't even know what soup he's eating. Good luck now." She pushed the door shut. A chain rattled. A lock clicked. Feet distantly walked away.

The wind lifted as I stepped off the porch, spinning some cherry blossom in circles. Looking back at the house, I saw a light come on in the front room, and then the elderly man's eyes appear between two slats of a horizontal plastic blind that he'd separated with his fingers. He pressed his nose against the glass, as if he was trying to get a closer look at me. The window steamed up around his face, making it look misty, withdrawn. For a moment, I saw my father: bald, twisted eyebrows, green eyes, bristly neck and shaving cuts dotting his heavy cheeks. I wanted to move forward and put my hand to the glass, wave to him, but as I was about to raise my hand, the nurse came up behind him and led him away by the waist. Even though I couldn't, I could hear the slats of the blind vibrate back into position, leaving behind a smudge of mist slowly evaporating on the window.

"No, this isn't it," I said, shaking my head at my mother as I joined her back at the gate that squeaked shut.

5.00 pm

"Google Maps is a wonderful thing, wouldn't you say?" the pharmacist turned to me as I stood next to her behind the counter. Positioning the cursor in the search box, she tapped the keyboard with her nail, typing ONE ENNIS ROAD, LIMERICK, not noticing that the caps lock was still on.

As she dropped her glasses onto her nose, peered closely at the monitor and used the roller ball of the mouse to zoom into the map, I noticed a bunch of prescription labels that were stuck to the sides of the screen. Reading them I could see that the pharmacy address also had no street number, as if this corner of Limerick had been forgotten. And below the address, a warning, in bold, 'keep out of sight and reach of children'. Was the label telling me that we shouldn't continue our search?

"Found it," she said.

The fan of a printer propelled into action. Lit by the screen, her face was heavily made-up and her smile was kind and hopeful. She flattened a colour print-out of the map showing the local area on a counter, and in the centre of the page circled number one Ennis Road in red ink. I could have searched for the address on my phone, but for some reason it felt more reliable asking the pharmacy for help, as if their local knowledge would get us closer.

She handed me the warm paper. Curled at one end, the ink was still damp and stained my fingertips. There it was, the childhood home of my Irish Jewish father with the words one Ennis Road, equidistant from Andrew's Garage, Shamrock Chinese Take-Away, Paul's Chimney Sweeping, and Noelle's Café, all labelled with icons denoting their trade. There was no icon for my father's home. I wondered what the icon would be for a house you can't find. A picture of a house with no roof, an empty plot of land, a question mark? Instead, a Google pin marked the address. I stared at the pin for a few seconds, trying to embed it into my mind, until it started to blink back at me, like a beacon.

"That's odd," I said.

"What's that?" she asked.

"That number one Ennis Road would be in the centre

of the map."

"Anything's possible around here, and who are we, after all, to second guess Google?" She looked at me over her glasses. "I'll just go and see to Sister Philomena…"

Returning to the map I focused at the URL printed at the bottom of the page. Equal signs, ampersands, hyphens, letters, numbers, question marks stretched off the edge, an infinite stream of possibilities. It made me think of all the elements that make up a memory, the sights, images, symbols that help us remember things. Maybe there was no horse, maybe the address is wrong, but does it matter? After all, maybe just seeing a glimpse of my father's childhood life in Limerick would do.

"So, come out of the shop, turn right, walk a few hundred metres on this side and, well, I'm pretty sure that's where it is," the pharmacist said.

"What's he after looking for?" the sister asked.

"The house his father grew up in, number one Ennis Road," she said. A few other waiting customers looked over at me.

"Do you know it?" I asked.

The nun smoothed her black habit with her hand. A string of rosary beads hung from her waist. "Who did you say lived there?"

"My father, a Jewish family, in the late 1930s."

"There's never been any Jews around here. Sure, they all lived over on Wolfe Tone Street, on the other side of the Shannon. Did you give me my insulin now, Deirdre?"

And with that my father came back to me. He also took insulin for his diabetes, and loved his weekly outings to the pharmacy: "something to do," he'd say, "and a pleasant walk." The pharmacy was his sanctuary, and I felt at that moment that he would have liked that we were asking for directions to his house there, amongst the bottles, pills, creams and perfumes.

An overhead heater warmed my head as the sliding doors of the pharmacy whooshed open. Blue sky trickled through the breaking clouds. I turned and looked up and down the road as if checking for traffic. Both sides were lined with houses, some stained by rain, others hidden by pine trees and gravel driveways. Nettles poked out through railings onto the narrow pavements, as if discouraging pedestrians. Rusting road signs hung from lampposts sign-posting long-finished trade shows and Fun World. We started to walk.

5.25 pm

We stopped in front of a grassy knoll that was dotted with dandelions and daisies. Broken bottles and cigarette ends circled the trunk of an oak tree next to a sign with the words 'Neighbourhood Watch Area'.

Across the road was a 1980s detached two-up, two-down. Stones filled the driveway, like a pebble beach, and an unevenly trimmed hedge covered a wall blocking the front window. A burglar alarm blinked over the front door. This couldn't be it, I thought.

My mother sat on a park bench as I approached the house nervously. A security spotlight clicked on, making me squint. The curtains in the front room twitched, and almost at the same time the front door opened.

Standing in the doorway was a heavy man in a t-shirt, shorts, trainers and ankle socks. I imagined him in the BMW that was parked on the road in front of the house driving to 'dad-rock'.

He had that look of someone who didn't have much to do.

"Can I help you?" he asked. His voice was hoarse.

"Excuse me, is this number one Ennis Road?" I asked.

His belly wobbled as he laughed. I wasn't sure why.

I unfolded the map the pharmacist had given me.

"Well," he said, "if Ennis Road *is* my address, then I've been wrong for more than twenty years."

"So what's your address?"

"'Dooneen', St James's Court. I don't know who's been spinnin' you fibs."

I refolded the map.

"Why do you want to know?" he asked.

"My father lived at number one Ennis Road when he was young, and, well, we thought we'd see if we could find it."

A heaviness swept over me and I began to feel that maybe we should give up. Did I expect my father, who'd been dead for five years, to open the door and greet us? Did I expect him to show us inside? Did I expect the house to look like a late 1930s family home? The fact was, I wasn't sure what to expect, but something made me go through the ritual of searching, as if I needed to experience the emptiness of not finding what I desperately wanted to get a glimpse of.

"Well," he sighed, "I'm off to the golf club now. Let's hope the rain holds off." He leant forward from the front door, glanced up at the sky, and held out his hand to check for rain.

"Where do you play?"

"Castletroy…"

"Oh, that's where my father and grandfather used to play. It says it here, in his book." I dug *Dream On* out of my backpack, fumbled for the right page, and read aloud: "*Tuesdays and Thursdays were sacrosanct golf nights, and most Sundays. The old man played at Castletroy, where I enjoyed the rare occasions he allowed me to caddy for him.*"

"When was that now?"

"1930s. They were a Jewish family."

"Sure I don't think we've ever had any of them in the club at all. Mind you, I'm not a historian, but I'd have known. I've played there for years. Listen, try going back down the road. There's a row of houses next to the Strand Hotel that might be the ones you're after. Right," he said, rubbing his hands together. "I best be off."

He slung a golf bag over his shoulder, slammed the front door, and walked across the driveway to the BMW, leaving me standing alone.

My feet sank into the pebbles as I stepped away from the porch.

"Not this one either," I said to my mother. "He said to try back down the road."

5.45pm

The name *Tír na nÓg*, Land of the Young, had been carved on a piece of slate screwed to a garden wall. Through the metal work of the gate, a path stretched alongside a front lawn that led to a red-brick Edwardian house at the end of a terrace. Detached from the Strand Hotel, it was the first house on Ennis Road. This must be it.

The door knocker clanged. A dog barked.

"Who is it?" a man asked as a blurred figure slowly came into focus through the mottled glass.

"Hi, is this number one Ennis Road?" I asked, talking at the door.

"One moment," he said. A lock clicked. A light switched on. The door opened.

A man in corduroy trousers and a check shirt stood in front of me. He was wearing slippers with furry rings around the ankles, and holding a newspaper in one hand and a black Labrador by its collar in the other. His hair was untidy, and looked as if I'd disturbed an afternoon snooze.

"Now, how can I help you?" he asked.

"I, we've been looking for number one Ennis Road. Is this it?" I said, my eyes wide, willing him to say yes.

"Well this house is called Tír na nÓg. Why do you want to know?"

The man up the road, I told him, had said that we should look at this row of houses. I went on that my father's unfinished memoir said that he'd lived at number one Ennis Road as a young boy, and that our family was Jewish, and that they'd moved to that house from Lansdowne Park, and I wanted to know if this was the right house. I stopped, but wanted to tell the man that while I knew that the house may not exist anymore, my father's unfinished memoir painted pictures in my mind of him standing in the doorway of a similar house as a young boy, in school shorts and shirt, his bare knees shivering in the cold, his blond hair parted, holding a satchel, my grandfather standing by his side, his golf bag packed and ready to go to Castletroy Golf Club.

"The Jews, they had a history with Limerick, didn't they?"

the man asked.

"Well, there were a few hundred of them here in the early 1900s."

"I seem to remember hearing about a pogrom or such like?"

"In 1904."

"That's it. Did many, you know, die?"

"Just one. My family was one of the few to stay. They moved to Dublin in the early 40s."

"Terrible story."

We pause.

"Well, you're a Limerick man then I suppose," he continued. "You're welcome to come in and take a look around if you'd like. There's not much to see, but…"

A few drops of rain spattered my jacket. I looked up to the sky and back at my mother.

"Thanks, but we need to catch the six-thirty bus," I said. "Thanks again, you've been…" I hesitated, as if I was scared to know if this really was the house, and maybe it would be better for things to be left unfinished, like my father's memoir. I started to walk back down the garden path.

"You do know that none of the houses around here have numbers," he called after me. "Just one of the strange things about Limerick…"

"I do," I said, as I snapped up my umbrella, and re-joined my mother at the gate.

6.30 pm

The bus pulled out of Limerick bus station into a threatening sky. I began to read chapter two of *Dream On*. It started, *Leaving Limerick, I can remember no goodbyes…*

The Bowl

Rob had five rules for a decent Saturday night out at south Dublin's Dundrum Bowl, the scene of many tragedies. Win at pool, get digits, snog and get served. And importantly, you had to stay on his wavelength.

These evenings were unpredictable, but they were an escape from drinking sherry from the bottle, while sitting on the wall by the Texaco garage with suicidal Jayo, or smoking joints in the back of Deco's car while he pulled hand-break turns on the gravel of the church car park, waiting for Father Doyle to ring his bell at them "feckin' lads in the car."

This particular Saturday, Rob was wearing his latest purchase, a copper-tan trench coat that reached his ankles and hung like a canvas tent over his squat body. Steel toe-capped Doc Martens stuck out from his feet like swollen tubes of liquorice. His hair was slicked back with Fudge hair gel, and he kept two curls dangling like slinkies over his forehead, which he frequently blew onto his head after he'd sucked them dry. A pair of jet-black jeans clung to his rugby-player thighs and plump arse, which he tried to conceal by stretching his jumper down over it every few minutes.

The 43. We'd waited many an hour in our teenage lives for the 43, a single-decker bus with worn cushioned seats that smoked with guff. Another rule, we had to get the right bus at the right time, otherwise we'd be late, and there'd be less time at the Bowl, and less time to score.

"43!" I shouted, as we turned the corner from Rob's street onto the main road. We legged after it, coming to a breathless stop as the bus sped past into the smog.

"Fuck," Rob shouted, his breath smoking in the cold night air, "it's already eight-fifteen." Another rule, rule number seven, don't be late. Broken. Not a good start.

"How much do you have?" he asked, as we continued towards the bus stop.

"Tenner," I said.

"Tenner? Is that all? Not enough to get a taxi then," he said, jabbing me in the shoulder.

"I'll get cash," I said, rubbing where he'd thumped my arm.

"I'll get cash," Rob sneered. "Come on, let's walk. My sources tell me that Aishling O'Reilly's gonna be there."

Rob set off, pounding the pavement, his oily hair shining like freshly laid tarmac under the streetlights, his coat flapping like a flag in the wind against the backs of his legs. I followed, always two steps behind, feeling stiff in my denim jacket, jeans and Converse boots, a cool sweat misting my forehead.

Half an hour later, we bounded onto a fetid 43. Rob sat next to an elderly woman with a few shopping bags next to her. I stood. Always the charmer, and to make space, Rob helped the woman move her bags. She thanked him, but he spent the rest of the journey smirking, making faces and nodding his head towards me, as if the whole situation was hysterical. I didn't find it particularly funny – she was just an old woman with some shopping bags – but for some reason, I joined in, making eye contact with him, pretending to laugh, giggling at nothing.

Looking out of the bus window as we passed the mental hospital in Dundrum, I wondered why I endured these nights with Rob. He was a tempestuous bastard; his father was the kind of dad who had a go at Rob in front of his friends, the kind of dad who played more with his dogs than with his son, the kind of dad who showed me how to pour a pint while telling me that I was doing a much better job than his son, the kind of dad who left Rob duty-free packets of M&Ms from business trips on the doorstep of his mum's house. Maybe I felt sorry for him, I don't know, but there was a mystery about him that intrigued me, and as I also didn't have anything better to do on these Saturday nights, I willingly tagged along, wondering if this night would be any different to all the other nights at the Bowl.

"Did you like her?" Rob asked, as we stepped down from the bus.

"What?"

"I saw you..."

"Yeah, she looked like your mum," I sniggered.

Rob pulled down his jumper and stomped across the car park towards a flashing neon bowling ball that was attached to the side of the warehouse-like building. The Bowl.

"How are ye?" Rob nodded to the bouncers.

"Any ID lads?" one of them wearing a high-vis jacket asked.

We took out our fake IDs, which the bouncer examined

with a torch, turning them over and feeling the plastic with his chubby fingers.

"Anything on ye?" he asked.

"Negative," Rob said. The two bouncers glanced at each other, bemused.

"No," I followed.

"Here you, negative boy, quick search."

The bouncer beckoned Rob's arms up and stretched his hands around the inside of his trench coat. Soon the bouncer was covered in the cloth of Rob's coat, before he emerged a few seconds later, stood up and smoothed his hair as the blood returned to his face.

"OK, no messin' lads," he said, letting us pass.

We entered a dark reception under flickering strip lighting, a smell of boiled sausages filling the air, our shoes sticking to the squidgy carpet. The sound of bowling balls cannoned against the walls like rolls of thunder, and the incessant tinkly sound of slot machines and arcade games reverberated around the low-ceilinged building.

"Two pounds entry," a girl with braces on her teeth and blonde hair tied in a bun said.

We paid, headed over to the bar and ordered two portions of chips and two pints of lager.

"Any ID?" a skinhead with a frayed shirt asked.

We flashed him our IDs.

"Not tonight lads."

"Wha?" Rob said.

"Look, they let you in, but I can't serve ye, alright?"

"But we come here all the time," Rob insisted.

He shrugged. "Nothin' I can do."

Another rule broken.

Rob sat at the front of the café that overlooked the pool tables still wearing his trench coat, as if he was holding court. I looked at him, his head moving from side to side, surveying his domain as he dunked his crinkly fries into blobs of ketchup and threw them into his mouth. Sliding down a plastic chair, I slurped a Coke and shook the ice around the hollow cup. We didn't talk.

Rob theorised that this was the most important part of the evening. If we got it wrong, we'd be stuck with the wrong girls or even worse, no girls at all. It was all in the waiting, he said. We had to wait, watch and see who was playing on which table, and then, at just the right moment, make our move.

"Shall we?" Rob asked.

"Yeah, I'll get the cues."

"Game of pool," I said to the barman.

"How many?" he asked.

"Two."

"Table four. Two-fifty."

I sensed Rob's eyes on me and turned to meet his gaze.

"Which table?" he mouthed.

I held up four fingers.

He strutted over to the bar eyeballing me.

"Not four, you dip shit, we need five, or even better seven."

"What? They're not here."

"They are. On six… come on."

Beyond the slot machines, I spotted Aishling O'Reilly and a friend giggling as she bent over a pool table, took aim with her cue and fired the white cue ball towards a colour.

139

We got two cues, balls and a square of blue chalk. Rob unbuttoned his trench coat, twisted his cue jiu-jitsu style around his back, and carried it like a sword in front of his body. He pulled his jumper down and walked towards table seven. He was ready.

"I'll break," I said.

"No you won't. I'll do it."

Rob walked around the table smiling broadly, and just before he broke, he paused and stretched back his shoulders, looked over at Aishling and her friend. They didn't look up from their game. Aishling was tall and skinny and her permed hair sat stiffly on her head, like frizzy dry pasta. She was pale and freckly, had a hairy mole on the side of her nose, and was wearing an unzipped white hoodie that showed off a cropped t-shirt.

Rob broke and spun around on his heels, the balls clattering against each other like tiny comets, before cushioning against the sides and coming to a stop on the green felt table.

I started to play, getting lucky every time I struck the ball. After a few minutes I'd cleaned up. We started a new game. Rob didn't get a look in. I wondered at some stage if I should let him win one, to make him feel better, but something in me wanted to test his nerve. I broke, and once again potted most of the balls, before he faulted and accidentally potted the black. My game. We continued for the next ten minutes. He stopped halfway through game three, put down his cue and took off his trench coat, carefully folding it and smoothing it onto a banquette.

Frustration steamed off him like a boiling kettle. As I played, he poked me in the arm with his cue in an effort to distract me. I didn't respond. He nudged the back of my cue just as I was about to take a shot, making me miss, so I set the balls up again.

He did it again, so I stared at him for a few moments. He did it again, and then burped in my face, before jumping aside, leaving a waft of vinegar lingering in the air.

"Fucking prick," I said, under my breath.

Rob played a double, potting a red, and looked around to see if anyone had noticed.

"Nice shot Robbie," Aishling said, sauntering over.

"Learnt all my tricks from him," Rob said.

"Game of doubles, lads?" she asked.

We left table seven and headed over to six. I purposefully chalked my cue, eager to play.

"You break, Murph," Rob said, now playing the nice guy.

I lined up the balls, removed the black plastic triangle and broke. The cue ball lifted lightly off the table before accelerating at speed, careering onto the spots and stripes. I stood admiring my break and watched as the balls came to a stop.

"Your go," Rob said to Aishling.

"Here Aoife, you go, I'm rubbish," she said.

Aoife stepped up and potted two stripes in quick succession, pivoting in her dirty Adidas trainers, and high-fiving Aishling after each shot. She had a widow's peak and dark hair that swept down over her black denim jacket, and dark red lipstick that made her lips shine against her white powdered face and black eyeliner, giving her an intriguing Goth look.

"Where did you learn to play?" I asked.

"Holiday," Aoife said.

"Where?"

"San Diego," Aoife said with an American accent.

"Oh, I'm half-American you know," said Rob, listening in.

141

Aoife ignored him.

"Yeah, it was cool, I have cousins there," she continued.

"Cool, did you go to Hollywood?"

"No, that's LA," she said, "but yeah, we went all over, and they play pool everywhere, so you just pick it up. Here, I'll show you."

She showed me how to bridge my fingers on the table, holding my hand with her nail-varnished fingers, and stood behind me to demonstrate how to position the cue accurately and visualise how to strike the ball.

"My secret weapon," Aishling laughed.

As Aoife and I played, Rob sat next to Aishling on the banquette, flicking his oily curls every so often with his head, his knee jerking up and down, up down, up down, up down. He inched closer to Aishling and turned to look at her, before resting his head on her shoulder like a needy child, and closed his eyes. Aishling let him rest there for a few moments before abruptly standing up and headed to the bar, leaving Rob alone sucking his ringlets of hair.

"How did you get served?" Rob asked Aishling incredulously, as she placed two pints onto the wooden edge of the pool table.

"I know the bar staff," Aishling said.

"Are ye done yet?" Rob asked standing up. Aoife and I ignored him. "Here. Give us the cue," he said.

"What?" I asked.

"Give us the fucking cue!"

"It's not your go…"

He snatched my cue, spun it aggressively, walked over to the table and started to fire balls randomly in all directions, licking his lips.

"Did you see that?" he asked. No one responded.

"Look at this, my secret weapon," he said, as he tried a shot behind his back, which failed to connect, the tip of the cue digging into the table, leaving a skid mark of blue chalk. We all laughed. Rob continued, belting the balls against the padded cushions, like thoughts rebounding inside the cell of his crazed mind.

"Rob get off, will you, it's not your go," Aoife implored.

"Did you see that?" he continued as he potted the white ball, took it out of the pocket, replaced it on the table, arranged the balls and broke again. Drips of sweat covered his forehead, his hair now shower-wet, his chest heaving.

"Jesus Robbie, will you stop…" Aishling shouted.

"This is fucking brilliant," he said, his eyes now wide open with amazement, as he ripped the threads of his jumper while pulling it further down over his legs.

"Rob, will ye…" I went over and put my arm on his shoulder and neck.

"Fuck off," he said, brushing away my arm and spinning his cue around his back. He caught one of the pint glasses, knocking it onto the table, letting the frothy lager slowly sink into the felt, leaving a mossy puddly mess.

"Come on Murph, let's go…" he said, beckoning to me.

"I'm not leaving," I said, moving my eyes towards Aoife.

"Well I'm not staying in this place, see ye later."

Aishling, Aoife and I stood still as Rob downed the other pint, unfolded and lubricated himself into his trench coat. He rolled his head from side to side until his neck clicked, felt into an inside pocket and took out one of his 'call me' cards that he'd recently had printed, and passed it to Aishling using both hands. He hesitated, looked at the three of us, sweat dribbling down the side of his stubble, and marched towards the exit.

"Jesus," I said, "see ye," and ran after him.

"Night lads," the bouncers said in unison as we left the Bowl into drizzle and walked towards the bus stop, our shoes squelching on the pavement.

"Did you see that? She was all over me…" Rob started up.

"What?" I asked.

"Suppose you like Aoife then…"

"Yeah, she's interesting."

"She's interesting," he repeated mockingly.

I shook my head.

This was how it always ended with Rob, in disappointment and accusation, but his self-destruction somehow made me feel alive, as if I was playing the role of co-star in a performance that he played out every time we went to the Bowl. But watching his tragedy play out suited me, as I knew that the next time I'd meet Aoife, she'd remember me, the normal friend, the one who tried to tame Rob, the interesting one.

I froze at the bus stop waiting for the last 43. Two girls walked up and started talking to us. I moved away, uninterested. Rob shared a cigarette with one of them, before she slowly disappeared inside his trench coat that he wrapped around her. The other one left them to it, as I slowly began to walk home.

The Butter Dish

The stage is set.

Dining room. An oak dining table. Benches on either side. Spotlights above the table. Rest of the dining room in semi-darkness.

"Two minutes." Actors are called.

Waiting in the wings I smell chicken soup. I hear feet moving through the house creaking on floorboards. I know we're getting close. I breathe.

Here we go. Lights. And. Action.

Four actors take their positions, sitting on the benches. Mother opposite Sister. Father opposite me. I'm never allowed to switch places.

"Stick something on," Father directs at me.

I almost forgot, it's my role to put on the music. Running my fingers across the spines of vinyl, I choose a suitably uplifting French Horn Concerto. Static lifts off the record as it slides out of its sleeve. The stylus drops gently onto the outer grooves and as it turns the Allegro of the orchestra lifts from the speakers, just in time for our first course.

I've practised you see. I am good at some things.

Tonight, like every other night, like every night for the last few years, we are ready. Music, lights, actors in position, and a performance to entertain our imaginary audience.

A hush descends as we unfold our napkins, and place them on our laps.

Scene One.

"Bread anyone?" Mother asks.

I grab a slice of bread and reach for the butter dish.

"Tidy it up, will you," Father says.

"What?" I pretend not to have heard.

"Tidy it up." This time sharply, without looking up from his bowl of scalding soup, just how he likes it.

He sits with a straight back, always on the edge of the bench, demonstrating to the rest of us how to sit upright. A man of few words, his slim frame and slight twitch of his head adds to his aura of unpredictability. His white shoulder-length hair glows in the soft light. A pair of gold-rimmed glasses cover his washing-up eyes. He's a loud sniffer, and likes to pick his nose with the sharp fingernail of his forefinger, before wiping his nostrils with the back of his hand.

"Tidy it up now," he says.

It takes me a moment to get ready. I stare at the butter dish that sits in the centre of the table on a tatty bamboo mat, sweating under the heat of the spotlights that glow like oven elements. The dish itself is small, has a square base with rough edges and a glossy round rim. Grease ripples from it onto the rough, biscuit-fired sides, adding to its sliminess.

Lift-off. This is the best bit of the play by the way, so watch and learn. A scene I've been rehearsing in minutiae.

"Why?" I ask, just to see if I can get away with not doing it tonight.

"Tidy *it* up, will you." No eye contact, brilliantly played. Critics love that part, so raw, so evocative of family life, they say.

The other actors lift their eyes to each other momentarily before returning to their soup, spoons knocking on bowls. Mother looks tired. Bags of memory and resignation fill her swollen eyes, scarred emotion ironed into her creased features.

Gripping the butter dish by its corners, I leave the heat of the main stage of the dining room, exit stage left to the hall and flick on the hallway light.

The stage moves with me.

I know I can jump the five steps down to the kitchen while holding the dish, so quickly slip off my trainers, stretch out my toes, wipe my pimply forehead with my other hand and set myself. I'm wearing my favourite red and black striped tracksuit top that feels tight on my arms, and leaves indentations on my wrists, but makes me feel like a proper sportsman. Peering down the five steps I lean back like a long-jumper in a starting stance, run and launch myself down the stairs still gripping the dish, landing perfectly with a triple jump onto the laminate floor.

I slide and steady myself in front of the cutlery drawer that I swish open and remove a bone-handled knife to 'tidy' the dish. I tackle the butter, pushing it down so that it's flat, even, pristine. In the past I've used a fork to give it that restaurant look and feel, where the butter is sometimes served cold, on ice, decorated

147

like a frilly ribbon, ready to be plundered and spread onto warm bread. He never complains then.

After smoothing, shoving and flattening, it looks presentable. But I need to finish it off, to give it my best shot, to get some kind of attention for my efforts. I also want a good review.

The problem is I've already been longer than I'd hoped, and the soup course is nearly finished. Mine will be cold anyway.

"What's going on?" a yell from upstairs.

"Coming…" I splutter.

To finish, I run a fork diagonally across the butter, signing-off my artistry. Tilting the dish in the light from side to side I admire my work and check for any irregularities. It's perfect.

No, I don't need applause, it's OK. I'll wait until the end of the performance, but thanks for asking.

I skid back across the kitchen, and run up the five steps, landing perfectly once again. The stage turns, and the lights shine back onto the dining room table. I wait for my fellow actors to notice my masterpiece. No one looks up.

"What took you? We've finished. I only asked you to tidy it up." No eye contact from the main star.

"I did tidy it up."

"I can see that, but what took you?"

I sit down at the table and rub my itchy feet together. My tracksuit sticks to me as I try and sit straight with my elbows by my side. My hair is matted to my forehead, and I just can't get the pulsating, pumping sound of the low, monotonous horn that emanates from the record player out of my head.

Who knows what my friends are doing right now? I'll never know. I've signed up for this open-ended contract for an unlimited run.

I still have to finish my soup, and now my dilemma – to butter or not to butter my bread? I slice a sliver and start spreading. The butter has loosened, and is now lovely and soft. It spreads easily, but perhaps it's because I'm hungry that I continue to dig into the dish until there are mounds of it on my bread. Gosh that's good I think, as I lick the butter and deeply bite into the slice.

My eyes back on the dish. What was pristine and perfectly manicured is now an explosion of yellow sludge.

He lifts his chin towards the dish.

"What?"

"Tidy it away."

I forgot, we can't have butter or bread with our main course. That's not how it's done, in civilised families.

End of scene one.

Scene Two.

It's my job to turn over the record. The Adagio, a slow start.

We sit for the main course. Silence descends on the table.

"What did you do today?" I direct my question at him. No response. He runs his bony hands through his silky hair. Mother and Sister sit in silence.

"What about that thing you said you were doing yesterday; you know the job you were working on?" I try again. "Did you finish the shoot in the studio?"

The sorrowful sounding horn lifts in volume, and starts to jar with the cutlery that clangs on the porcelain plates. We cut and scrape our food.

"Can we put more salt in the food," he says with a mouthful, not looking at anyone in particular. "It's bland."

"There you go," Mother says, as the salt gets passed across the table.

He sticks his fingers into the pot of salt, and sprinkles a hefty pinch over his food. Straightening his back, his head twitching like a flickering light, he gazes at me for a moment. Is he about to say something? The horns speed up. Nothing. Another twitch, and he looks straight back down at his plate.

"So was Mick your assistant today?" I ask, my hands clammy. "He's funny, always pinching me whenever I come along. Really like him. And he told me about the time he went to Old Trafford and saw Frank Stapleton," I gabble on, stuffing food into my mouth. "I like him and the other guy, Nick, is it? He's cool. He always wears those massive gloves. He looks like the Michelin man. Was he there today? And Marcie. She was telling me, last time I saw her that is, about the time she took Rory canoeing and they all fell in the canal. Mind you they nearly drowned, so I suppose it wasn't that funny, I haven't seen him in ages. Is she still working with you?"

He places his knife and fork heavily onto his plate, creating a hollow, startling sound.

"Look." Pause. The script is so well-developed here. "Listen," he looks across the table at me, "will you stop, just stop asking me so many questions," he barks.

My mouth now seems to be panting along to the French horn, pumping its low melody from its spaghetti-like brass pipes, note after note, the octaves rising and falling, as the tune tumbles over itself in my head.

The feeling we've created here after so many years is magical. I have to create a sense of not knowing anything that's going on, as if I'm too young to understand. That's what he said when we rehearsed all those years ago. You're too young to really understand what's going on. Don't worry, when you're older you'll look back on these performances because they will set you up for life, perhaps a career in the theatre. I believed him then, as I do now. I'm too young. Everyone else seems to understand, but no one says anything, so neither do I.

My bony bum has gone numb from sitting on the wooden bench. I shift my body so as to avoid the rusty screws and nuts that poke out of the table, holding the cuts of wood together. I stay still and eat methodically, trying my best to not lick my knife or use my fingers to eat.

End of scene two.

Scene Three.

The Crescendo starts, the movement we've all been waiting for. The finale.

As dessert is served, Father takes off his glasses, shoves back his plate, knocks back the dregs of a glass of wine and just like that throws his napkin onto his plate of food. It lands softly, making little impact, but the dramatic skill makes me jump. Standing up, he looks around, wanting us to notice his climatic scene. But we don't. We just sit still, because we know what happens next, because it happens every night. The script never changes, the

151

scenes are always the same. A long run this one.

He moves stage left and snags a belt buckle of his jeans on the screw on his side of the table. "Shite," he mutters under his breath, before releasing himself. The leaning bookshelves behind us sway slightly, as he shuffles slowly across the worn carpet towards the exit. He grabs the doorknob on the wooden door, pulls it open and departs.

What. A. Performance.

The spotlights follow him to the bathroom. He switches on the light and dunks two soluble tablets into a worn plastic mug. He gulps it back, like a shot of whisky, and sits on the toilet, no doubt reflecting, analysing tonight's performance, thinking what he can do to improve the next night.

Mother leaves the table as the lights focus on me. My back is now aching from sitting on the bench, so I lie down on the bench for a few minutes and stare up at the spotlights that are above the table, until oily light-streams fill my eyes and tears start to roll down the side of my face. I blink to try to get rid of the sensation, but it lingers, explosions of colours blurring my sight.

Mother returns as the lights fall back on the table.

"He'll be back soon. Eat up," she says.

I make space for her on the bench and put my head on her warm soft lap, yearning for comfort. It's dark and warm there. I once asked her if I could hide down here, maybe even live here, where it's hidden from everyone and everything else, where I don't have to de-grease the butter dish on a daily basis, where I don't have to turn over the record, where I don't have to perform. No, I was told. You are critical to the performance; we need you.

As I sit up, my eye comes level with the screw on my side of the table. I stare at it closely, admiring its power, its strength, its sharpness. I move my eye as close as I can to the screw so that it's now directly in front of me, completely filling my vision. One tiny move and my eyeball will be perforated. Maybe that would shift the audience's attention from him to me. Maybe then I'll get the plaudits I deserve.

I gradually move my eye away and sit up, blood draining from my head. I place my knife and fork on my plate. None of us have noticed that the last movement of the concerto – the Crescendo – has stopped. All I can hear is the hum of the stylus on the centre of the record.

Father walks back onto the main stage and returns to his place at the dining table and sits down opposite me. He looks at me over his glasses and winks, as if everything is OK.

Curtain.

Acknowledgements

There are many people who have helped me with my writing – too many to mention here - but I should thank my editor Dominic Wakeford, writing mentor Zoe Gilbert and publisher and friend Goran Baba Ali. The writing community is incredibly supportive and I'm grateful that I am part of such a generous group. My writing is influenced by my life and memories and those that I share my life with, but it's those closest to me that deserve most of my thanks, including my children, my mother, who proofed my work and of course my best critic, perfect partner and loving wife Miriam. Thank you.

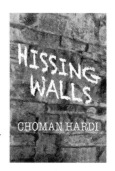